UAV

Book I in the
Horizon's Wake series

A Novel By
Lincoln Cole

This is a work of fiction. Names, characters, organizations, places, events, and incidents are either products of the author's imagination or used fictitiously. Any resemblance to actual persons, living or dead, or actual events is purely coincidental.

No part of this work may be reproduced, or stored in a retrieval system, or transmitted in any form or by any means, electronic, mechanical, photocopying, recording, or otherwise, without written permission of the publisher.

Published by Lincoln Cole, Columbus, 2015
LincolnJCole@gmail.com
www.LincolnCole.net

Cover Design by M.N. Arzu

Reviews for *UAV*

"This book is fast-paced and action-packed, with multiple interesting twists."
   Valerie Thomas, author *of Auburn*

"UAV is reminiscent of a James Rollins adventure, and I found myself staying up with it into the night, until I finished it."
   Richard Becker, author of *The Catch*

"No price is too high. In a game of high stakes there will be casualties."
   Ian Welch, author of *Target*

Table of Contents

Chapter 1 9
Chapter 2 29
Chapter 3 45
Chapter 4 49
Chapter 5 57
Chapter 6 65
Chapter 7 77
Chapter 8 81
Chapter 9 89
Chapter 10 91
Chapter 11 97
Chapter 12 105
Chapter 13 121
Chapter 14 127
Chapter 15 131
Chapter 16 141
Chapter 17 147
Chapter 18 151
Epilogue 157

"It has become appallingly obvious that our technology has exceeded our humanity."

Albert Einstein

Chapter 1
Lahore, Pakistan

1

"Do you think they are staring at us because of how we smell?" William asked.

Victor Cross blinked, wondering if he should laugh or groan. He was sitting on a park bench outside the Siddiq Trade Center in Lahore, Pakistan, twirling a pair of Chanel sunglasses in his hand and trying to appear inconspicuous; a task made all the more difficult by his bumbling compatriot.

"What?" Francis asked from the opposite side of the bench, just as confused as Victor.

"You know," William explained, "like hamburgers. Do you think we smell like hamburgers?"

Victor decided groaning was the proper response.

"What the hell are you going on about?" Francis reiterated. "Why would we smell like hamburgers?"

Francis was Victor's second in command, the only person Victor would trust with his life. Unlike William, Francis Umstead was lithe, standing barely over five feet and thin as a rail. His accent was thick cockney, hard to understand until enough time had been spent with him, and he wasn't at all intimidating to look at.

His size was deceptive, though, and Victor would prefer facing William, the three-hundred-pound bull of a man, in a fight over Francis. Francis was the most brilliant tactician Victor had ever met, and he knew every dirty trick for disabling and crippling opponents.

While Victor built his reputation and became famous as an international mercenary for hire, Francis was always there at his side keeping him out of trouble. They both worked for

JanCorp, a mercenary company that ran jobs for governments, corporations, and private citizens. Francis was brilliant and dangerous.

William, on the other hand...

"You know, like in that movie," William elaborated, completely missing Francis's objection. "The one where soldiers keep eating Chinese food so they don't smell like Americans when they sneak in to shoot people. These people keep staring at us, and I was wondering if it's because we smell like strange food to them. Like it's seeping out of our pores or something?"

"Do you ever run out of stupid things to say?" Francis asked.

"No joke, man, all the attention is starting to creep me out," William replied. He was staring at the passing crowd and tapping the side of his leg. His gun was strapped there, beneath the robes.

"Don't do that," Victor said casually. "No sense drawing attention to yourself."

"Okay, boss," William said, folding his arms.

It was an oppressively hot day in the Lahore, Pakistan, and Victor couldn't stop sweating. Places he hadn't even known *could* sweat were swampy and uncomfortable.

He was less worried about his own comfort, however, and more about his gear: heat was brutal on electronics, and too much time in the sun could fry the hardware. His laptop sat open on the bench beside him, and he was using it to monitor the timeline and details of his plan.

Francis stirred beside him, glaring over at William.

"You don't think they might be avoiding us maybe because you're a gigantic freak?" Francis asked.

William continued, keeping his voice low and ignoring Francis. "I mean, you wonder if they can smell meat on our clothing or something. Do you think it makes them mad since cows are sacred?"

Francis stood in stunned silence, and Victor couldn't help

but laugh. A minute passed as Francis sought a reply.

"That's Hinduism, you moron," Francis said breathlessly. "These are Muslims."

William hesitated. "Oh."

"In his defense, we *just* left India," Victor offered.

"When's the last time you even *ate* a hamburger?" Francis asked. "Just how long do you think it stays in your system?"

William was red-faced and confused. He didn't take taunting well.

"I was only wondering..."

"They are on schedule," Victor said, ending the conversation and closing the laptop. "We have a little under two minutes."

"Why do they want him alive?" William asked. "It would be a lot easier just to kill Imran."

"That isn't our job," Victor said.

"They want to hold him responsible for his crimes," Francis added.

"What crimes?" William asked. He shifted. "The guy hasn't even done anything yet."

"No," Victor agreed. "But the people would follow him if he asked. So they are going to hang him publicly and make an example of him for everyone to see."

"Won't that just make people hate their leaders even more?"

"That isn't our concern," Victor replied. "Our job is clear: take Imran alive. Whether or not they kill him isn't our concern."

"Helen won't like that," Francis said softly, looking pointedly at Victor.

He gave Francis a long look. "Helen doesn't need to know. As far as she's concerned, Imran is getting a fair trial."

"Of course," Francis replied smoothly. "Do you think she knows?"

"She doesn't have the slightest clue," Victor said.

"And what if she figures it out?"

"Then I'll take care of it," Victor replied. "Wouldn't be the first time."

Victor's phone buzzed in his pocket. He glanced up at the streetlights around him. It was the middle of the day in bright sunlight, but those lamps were flickering to life with a telltale yellow glare. It was their cue from the fourth and hidden member of their team that the convoy was under a minute away.

"That's our signal," he said, closing the laptop and standing up from his bench, "time to work."

2

Helen Allison typed a sequence of commands into her keyboard and glanced out the window at the street below. She was on the third floor of the Siddiq Trade Center, overlooking Jail Street where Victor and the rest of the crew were assembled.

She was average height, attractive if a bit skinny, with brunette hair and soft features. She rarely bothered to wear makeup or fix up her hair because she spent most of her time with computers.

She was also the newest member of Victor's team, this being only her second time out in the field. She had worked with Victor before while contracting with JanCorp as a hacker, but from a distance usually in a lab with other analysts. Those jobs had also taken place while her sister was alive.

She had offered to join Victor out in the field because he had been the one running the operation when her sister was killed two weeks ago. There hadn't been a lot of information released to Helen from JanCorp about exactly what happened, nor any pictures or body. Only a report that her sister was dead from an explosion. Helen wanted to know what had happened to her big sister, and no one seemed to know outside of Victor's team.

Maybe, if she got close enough, she could get the truth.

For now, she would play along, pretend to be oblivious, and get her answers.

She glanced out the window and tried to locate Victor or Francis in the sea of people. They were somewhere below. Had they seen the lights? She hoped so because none of the team were in her view. All she could see was a throng of locals going about their daily lives like nothing was wrong.

How many will die today?

She didn't want to think about that. If things went well, none would. Not civilians, anyway.

Her phone started ringing. She glanced at it, then clicked the connect button.

"Mom, this isn't a good time."

"Helen," her mother said. "Where were you?"

"I've been working," Helen replied. "I couldn't make it."

"You couldn't make it to your own sister's memorial service?"

Helen felt a tightness in her chest. "I was busy."

"You're still working for that company, aren't you? You promised your sister that you would quit."

"I know," Helen said. "But there isn't much point in that now, is there?"

"She didn't want this life for you," her mother said. "I don't either."

"We don't want a lot of things," Helen said. "I need to—"

"Is this how you honor her memory, by risking your life like she did? You always looked up to her, but that's no excuse for getting yourself killed."

Helen was silent for a moment. When she spoke, her voice was icy. "There was no reason for her to get herself killed either. Look where that got us?"

"Helen…"

"Mom, I need to go," Helen said, hanging up the phone.

She let out a deep breath and tried to clear her mind, pushing the concerns away. She felt unsettled with an aching feeling in her stomach. It had been two weeks since her sister had been killed, and she hated being reminded of it. Her older sister, her perfect sister, her dead sister.

She pushed the thoughts away. She needed to focus on work.

Down the road less than a quarter of a mile away was the approaching convoy. The vans were bulletproof and insulated, with the sole intention of transporting Imran Hyderi safely through the city of Lahore to an important business meeting.

She didn't know what Imran's meeting was about. Didn't want to know.

This would be Imran's first trip into civilized territory in six weeks, and there was no telling when he might reappear if they missed him today.

She was out of radio contact with her team—Imran's convoy traveled with jammers that blocked electronic communication within a half mile—so she would have to trust that they held up their end of the plan. Her job was to hack the security systems of this shopping center, disable the power grids and set off fire alarms.

With luck and a little encouragement, panic would ensue and civilians would flood the streets. After a few seconds, she would reroute power, turn everything back on, and cover any trace she'd been mucking around in their security system. Certain people would know that the system was hacked, but the government would play it off as a random system glitch.

Helen was depressed with how easy this job was turning out to be. She had a toolkit with wires and connectors to hack directly into an internal feed if that was necessary. She thought, at least, the critical systems would be off the grid.

Instead, she'd managed to hack the entire system through Wi-Fi from a coffee shop on the second floor. Her tools sat unused, and the entire hack had taken under thirty seconds. A simple script she downloaded from the Internet had gotten through all of their firewalls using backdoor proxy servers and web kits. It made her feel like a script kitty.

The rest of her time waiting consisted of a bagel and two

cups of Turkish coffee to stave off nervousness.

Two cups, it turned out, had been a bad idea. Now she was writhing in her chair, afraid to leave her post.

"Come on, come on, come on," she groaned, bracing herself for the ensuing power outage and blaring alarms. She didn't enjoy loud and repetitive noise, so she was as far from the speakers as she could position herself. "Hope you boys are ready."

With an anticipatory grimace, she typed the activation command into her laptop.

3

The streetlights turned off again, but that was the only sign that anything was amiss during the first few seconds. Most of the civilians didn't notice the streetlamps at all, and only a few glanced over as Victor and Francis meandered away from the benches toward the roadway.

William had disappeared into the shopping center a few moments earlier, milling near the sliding front doors and waiting for his moment to push them down.

The convoy was in sight now, less than two hundred meters away. If Helen blew the alarm too early, the caravan would stop and detour down another street. If she blew it too late, the reinforced and defensible vans would slip past before there were obstacles in place to hinder them. In either scenario, they would have no hope of capturing Imran. Timing was everything.

A little more than one hundred meters away, Victor heard the alarms blaring from inside the shopping center. He watched the approaching vans out of the corner of his eye and turned his attention to the sliding doors behind him. They were sensor operated, and without power couldn't function, but they were built on safety hinges for disasters.

Pushed off the hinges, they would swing safely out of the way. Victor was certain that civilians would figure out how to open the doors eventually on their own, but right now he didn't have time to wait. That was where William came in.

A group of confused people milled at the door. A few seconds after the alarms began, William pushed the glass door in a rush, knocking the sliding doors off of their hinges and escaping into the sunlight outside.

Victor noted with dismay that only one doorway swung open and the other hung at an angle, blocking passage.

Behind William in the mall, civilians were milling in a state of uncertainty, but when they saw the large man knock open the emergency exit their confusion shifted to fear.

They swarmed outside through the single door, but Victor knew the stream of people wouldn't be fast enough. He needed more, and the small opening with only one doorway had turned into a bottleneck. They were afraid but only afraid enough to go outside. No one was panicking.

Not yet, at least.

"Stop the convoy," Victor mumbled to Francis, walking toward the open door. He pushed through the oncoming crowd, fighting into the mall. Hundreds of people were vacating stores and filling the antechamber, confused.

The vans were close, and without more people rushing into the streets, Imran would disappear past without any problem.

Francis nodded and turned to face the road, pulling his hood up to cover his face. Victor fought to the double doors of the shopping center, grabbing the blocking door and yanking it out of the way.

He began waving his hands and pointed frantically at the windows above them.

"*Aag!*" he shouted in Punjabi.

"*Nar!*" he added in Arabic, just in case some shoppers weren't local. "*Aag Lagana!*"

At the declaration of *fire*, confusion shifted to terror, and seconds later other people were screaming as well. It took Victor only seconds to incite real panic among the shoppers, but those were precious seconds he hadn't expected to waste.

He wasn't worried, though, not yet. They might have to improvise, and he had to hope something would present itself. Victor slipped through the crowd and worked his way back to the edge of the road.

He picked his target out of the line of oncoming vehicles. He was responsible for neutralizing the third van in line, but he was fairly certain it wasn't the one Imran would be traveling in. The delegate would be in the middle or front van.

Victor scanned the crowd for Francis as he moved down the street. The convoy was fast approaching and right now it would have no difficulty bypassing the impromptu blockade of milling civilians.

He caught a momentary glance of his second in command, ducking in the crowd near the edge of the street. He hoped Francis had a plan to stop the vehicles, or this would all be for nothing.

Whatever he is doing, Victor thought, he'd better do it fast.

4

"*Where is your mother?*" Francis asked in Punjabi, kneeling next to a young child and speaking slowly.

His dialect was precise but unpracticed, and he was forced to enunciate the words to ensure she would understand. The little girl was terrified, and Francis felt bad for what he was about to do.

Bad, but not enough to stop. She was young, between five and seven years old, and had no idea what to do in this situation. And, of course, things were worse for her than they should have been: Francis had circumvented the crowd as it dispersed outside the broken doors, separating this young girl from her mother and guiding her several dozen feet away without anyone becoming aware.

Now she was lost, disoriented, and wanted nothing more than to find her mother. Francis heard the mother in the distance as the crowd dragged her along in the undercurrent, begging to be reunited with her child.

Unfortunately, that wasn't what Francis had on his agenda. His plan relied on the humanity and generosity of his enemy. Woe to this girl if they didn't have any.

Imran Hyderi was important to the people of his country because of his nobility and honor. He was among the heroes and saviors who would not resort to violence and preached peace. The last thing such heroes wanted to do was associate themselves with the tactics and mannerisms of their opposition. As such, they would surround themselves with people of similar ilk.

He'd chosen this young girl because the drivers were more likely to stop from hitting a child who wandered into their path than an adult. The girl was scanning the gathered crowd for her mother, tugging at the little Bhurka covering her hair.

Francis timed it perfectly, letting the vans come close enough that they would have to swerve and stop rather than change course, then pointed across the street and gave the little girl a push.

"*There's your mother!*" he said, and the little girl didn't hesitate. She ran into the middle of the street, shouting for her mother, oblivious to the black vehicles barreling down on her.

Several people started screaming, and Francis stepped into the roadway behind the little girl, pretending as if he was trying to stop her.

He was careful to stay far enough back that if the driver *did* decide to run the girl over, the van wouldn't come close enough to clip him too.

His gamble paid off, however, and the sound of screeching tires filled the air as the front driver slammed on the brakes. The van swerved, and the smell of burnt rubber filled his nose.

The little girl screamed and fell on her butt, staring at the engine block coming to a halt less than three feet from her face.

Only seconds later the street was filled with dozens of pedestrians, surrounding the girl and the now stopped line of vehicles. Some shouted angrily at the drivers; others shouted to find out what was going on.

Francis disappeared back into the crowd and maneuvered to the second van in line. Victor didn't have Intel on which vehicle Imran was traveling in, so the plan was to sneak a view into the interiors of each and eliminate the ones they didn't need.

It wouldn't do any good to attack from the outside: the van exterior was armored against small bombs and bullets up to fifty caliber by armor plates. Anything sufficient to stop the convoy would likely kill everyone inside.

But to save weight and cost, the interior was not compartmental or fortified. Once a door opened, all of the outer defenses were for naught.

He adjusted his loose fitting thobe to hide his movements as he drew a Colt revolver. As predicted, the passenger door opened and a guard climbed out, waving a gun and shouting in Punjabi for the crowd to disperse. Francis readied to shoot if the man moved to close the door behind him, but luckily it was left open.

The guard was armed with an assault rifle—a modified AK— and he was using the barrel to encourage civilians to step away from the van and clear a path.

Francis shifted nearer to the passenger door, cocking back the hammer on his revolver and pulling a tear gas grenade from another pocket. The crowd was getting more and more chaotic, and the guards were having no luck pushing them away from the vans.

The crowd was also growing in size as more and more surprised shoppers flooded out of the mall. Francis moved into position next to the passenger door.

He found an angle to peer across the front seat of the van, and with practiced ease fired off two rounds into the driver in rapid succession, tossing the tear-gas grenade into the backseat. It all happened in less than two seconds, and Francis ducked back into the crowd again before the guard in the street knew what had happened.

The civilians screamed and thrashed about, struggling to get away from the gunshots. A few pointed at Francis, but no one moved to hinder him as he shifted through the gathering.

He heard more gunshots from in front of and behind him in the roadway as Victor and William took out the other vehicles.

He ignored them and focused on his own job. He slipped around the far side of the van, next to the rear sliding door, and waited. A few seconds later it opened and gas billowed into the air.

Two men stumbled out, coughing and covering their faces with clothing. Francis fired two more shots, and both men collapsed to the ground. Then he moved forward into the interior of the van overtop them, avoiding the noxious gas, and peered inside.

It was empty. Francis let out a sigh. It wasn't practical for Imran to be in the middle van, but he had to check nevertheless. William was working the first van and Victor the last, and Francis knew that if one of them needed help, it would be William.

He reached into his pocket for more ammunition and saw the last guard stepping around the corner of the van. He'd recovered quicker than Francis expected and was raising his rifle to fire.

Francis dove toward the rear of the van, scrambling out of sight just as the rifle went off. He heard bullets thud around him and knew several civilians were hit in the barrage.

Francis crawled to the far side of the van and rolled underneath, facing toward the rear of the undercarriage. He watched the guard's feet as they rounded the van at the back. Francis fired, hitting the man in the right ankle.

The man collapsed to the ground with a scream, and as a soon as his head came in sight below the undercarriage Francis fired again, planting a bullet in his skull. Francis continued rolling through to the far side of the van, opening the cylinder on his Colt revolver and letting the empty shells spill onto the pavement.

He started to stand up, pulling more shells out of his pocket to reload. Things were progressing smoothly, and with a few more minutes they would be on the road with their target long before any response could be mustered against—

He saw the foot coming at the last second and managed to shift his neck far enough to avoid the brunt of the attack. The shoe caught him in the shoulder instead of the chin, knocking him against the van and sending a wave of pain down his spine. He fought to maintain control of his senses and spotted the man in front of him, stepping back and shouting.

The attack caught him off guard. His brain went into overdrive determining the ramifications.

Francis hadn't anticipated civilian intervention during this mission, and he knew that if he miscalculated his next move, things could turn from simple to desperate in a matter of seconds. If one civilian decided to join the fray and attack the outsiders, what would others do?

He couldn't afford for the crowd to turn into a mob. Francis shifted his weight underneath him as the assailant readied a second kick and noted with dismay that more civilians were moving to join in.

They were emboldened by the first attacker's success. This could get out of hand, and if he let these people enter into mob mentality his team would be in a lot of trouble. He slipped one shell out of his pocket, spilling a few live rounds on the pavement in the process, and slid it into the chamber of his revolver.

He snapped the cylinder into position and waited. One shot was all he would get, so he would need to make it count.

Only a second before the kick came he sprang into motion, stepping forward and catching the leg of the assailant with his left hand. He stood up and threw the man backward.

The attacker collapsed against another person and formed a heap in the center of the road, but Francis ignored them. He studied the crowd carefully, selecting a man who seemed likely to join the fray from those still hesitating.

The man wasn't aggressive yet, but he was big and strong. Francis knew it was only a matter of time. The crowd was building fervor now, ready to protect themselves against the outsiders, and that was something he couldn't afford.

Francis didn't hesitate, raising his Colt and firing his shot. The would-be assailant collapsed to the ground, half his head missing, and the crowd fell silent. The fervor was gone in the blink of an eye. Many were splattered in blood and gore. Many more seemed shocked as they stared at Francis.

He hadn't shot the man that attacked him, but instead an innocent bystander. *Who the hell does that?* The question was written on their faces, and they understood that this wasn't their fight. The mob mentality was gone, and now they were all afraid and isolated again. Francis calmly reloaded more shells into his revolver and stared back at them.

"*Anyone else?*" he asked in Punjabi.

There was no response, and he started walking toward the van parked in front of his. The crowd parted before him, silenced by his display of brutality. These were civilians, not trained to operate under battle conditions.

Or maybe it wasn't me that stopped them, he realized suddenly. His display of brutality was nothing compared to his compatriot's. The civilians were giving an even wider berth for William without the man needing to make any display.

William was leaning against the edge of his van, panting heavily and dripping in blood. It wasn't his. There was a man on the ground in front of him, tied up and with a cloth bag pulled over his face. Most impressive—and nauseating—was the crowbar he held in his right hand. The crowbar was, also, dripping blood.

"Where did you find a crowbar?" he asked.

William held it up for inspection, as though surprised to see it in his hand. "I'm not really sure...must have been in the backseat."

"Was it necessary?"

William shrugged. "Probably."

Francis shook his head. He gestured to the tied up man on the ground next to William. "Is he injured?"

"He's fine. He was begging earlier."

"He isn't now?"

William shrugged. "I kicked him in the face. He tried to rouse the civilians against us, kept asking for people to fight for him."

"I don't think that's going to be an issue," Francis replied, glancing back at the terrified crowd. "Is the van damaged?"

William shook his head. Everything was quiet, and a moment later Victor pushed through the crowd to join them. "I rigged the others to explode. We need to leave before these people realize they can swarm us."

Victor and William lifted Imran into the van, dragging the dead men out and dropping them onto the pavement. Francis was a little disgusted to see that only one man was shot while the rest received death-by-crowbar. It was embarrassing and barbaric, but there was nothing he could do about it now.

"I didn't want to damage the engine, boss," William explained. "So I tried not to use my gun."

"Good plan," Victor said. Francis could detect a slight undertone of sarcasm, but he knew it would pass over William's head.

"In less than a minute, there will be a large explosion here," Francis said, addressing the crowd in Punjabi. They stared at him blankly. "Anyone who stays or tries to stop us will die."

He climbed into the driver's seat of the van and fired the engine. He used his sleeve to wipe enough blood off the windshield to see out and decided he would have a talk with William later. *Sometimes a little finesse is necessary.* The crowd parted as he inched forward, and in only a few minutes they were on empty roads heading east.

"Will anyone follow us?" William asked.

Victor shook his head. "Not a chance. The civilians can't

respond to the incident, and the military is loyal to the national leaders."

"What happens now?"

"Now," Victor started, "we leave Imran at the drop point and disappear."

"I mean here," William said. "What we just did."

Victor leaned back into his seat. "The military releases a report, some people get mad and write letters or stories about cruelty and horror, and the government's opposition disappears for a few more years."

"You're wrong," a foreign voice said, and it took Francis a moment to realize that it was Imran speaking, tied up on the floor of the van. The voice spoke clear English, though with a distinct accent.

"You didn't gag him?" Francis asked, glancing over his shoulder. William shrugged.

"Kicking him was easier."

"We will never disappear," Imran said, but he didn't try to sit up from his prone position.

"All evidence to the contrary," Francis said.

"You mock something you know nothing about."

"You are a prisoner tied in the back of your own escort van being handed over to a man who will kill you, perhaps publicly. What else is there to know?"

"My death means nothing. We fight for the people. For freedom. Something you have and yet deprive others of. You will never understand what it is like to have something to fight for. Something to die for."

"Maybe not. But I like to think there is *nothing* worth dying for. I might not have conviction, but I always win."

"Then you don't understand that you already lost the only battle that counts," Imran said.

Francis shrugged. "Yeah, whatever."

5

Victor walked into the field of sugar cane outside the military base in Eastern Pakistan. Imran Hyderi was now in the custody of the government, and he neither knew nor cared what they would do with him. His team was back inside the operation tent, packing their gear and belongings.

Helen was annoyingly hyper and continually retreating to the restroom. He would have to remember to keep her away from Turkish coffee in the future.

Francis found him outside the tent. Victor could tell there was something on his mind.

"What's wrong?"

"What happens when she finds out?" Francis asked.

"About Imran?"

"About her sister," Francis replied.

"She won't," Victor said, waving the concern away.

"She's smart," Francis said, "and persistent. She isn't going to give up."

"No," Victor said. "But she's soft. She has none of the iron her sister had. She'll be easy to break."

"Do we need to break her?"

"What do you mean?"

"I mean, is this worth it? Why don't we just cut her loose and get someone else."

Victor was silent for a moment. "You said yourself that she isn't going to stop looking for answers. When she finds them, I would prefer that she be close enough that I can deal with it. Her sister had a lot of friends. If Helen told the right people what we did..."

"Things could get messy," Francis finished. Victor nodded.

"She doesn't know anything yet. When she starts to figure it out, I'll have a bullet ready for her."

Francis eyed his boss for a second, nodded, and then walked away. Victor watched him leave. He started walking back toward the military outpost when his phone started ringing.

"This is Cross."

"There's been a change of plans. We need you stateside," the voice said. He didn't recognize it: JanCorp cycled phone representatives. Worst case scenario, he could pick one voice out of a lineup at most. "We have our opening."

And it didn't matter anyway. He didn't plan on letting a worst case scenario ever find him. He hung up the phone and began meandering back to his crew. Only one thing mattered right now.

They had a job.

Chapter 2
Nevada

1

"Did you get the peyote?" Beck asked.

Jack Wallis wasn't even through the door of the double-wide trailer. He couldn't immediately answer since he held a bag of Doritos clenched between his teeth.

It was just past midnight, but neither of them were even the slightest bit tired. They were night owls, working into the early morning hours and sleeping during the day.

Jack made his way over to the counter of their drab little kitchen, weaving around desks and garbage. He dumped his bounty of processed foods, potato chips, and beverages down before turning to answer.

"Did I get the what?"

"The peyote," Steve Beck replied.

"I thought you were going to clean up while I was gone."

"I did," Beck replied. He had a switchblade in his hand and a whetstone on his lap. He eyed the edge and ran the blade down the stone. "So, did you get it?"

Beck was a scrawny twenty-six-year-old albino from Kentucky, barely over a hundred pounds. What he lacked in muscle he made up for in lung capacity.

Beck was smart, though; certainly a lot smarter than Jack, which he didn't have a problem admitting. And Jack wasn't dumb, anyway. He just felt dumb around Beck.

Beck was a commissioned officer in the United States Air Force, the same as Jack, but well on his way to becoming a Captain. He was technically Jack's superior, but rank didn't mean much out here in the middle of the Nevada desert.

The only nearby town, Dover, was twenty miles away.

They were isolated from civilization. The only contact with the outside world—apart from the occasional excursions into town for snacks at a gas station—were when they operated Predator drones flying around the world on a mission.

To make matters worse, they were operating drones from a mock retirement community barely thirty miles outside the Vegas Strip. So close to that majestic city, yet it might as well have been on the moon. It sat in the distance, mocking them in their double-wide in Olde Pine Trailer City.

There were well over two hundred trailers parked here, but less than half were occupied. Fewer drones in the air meant fewer pilots, and all branches of the military were working with contractors as the technology matured.

Jack put a twelve pack of Coke into the mini fridge.

The clock beeped, signaling that their shift was about to start.

"What the hell is Peyote?" Jack asked, opening the bag of Doritos and popping the tab on one of the cans. It was still warm, but he was thirsty.

"You're kidding, right?" Beck asked.

He was reclining on the couch in the southern corner of the room. "I told you where to go, who to talk to, and how much to ask for. Did you even *look* at the paper I sent with you?"

"Uh...no. Not really. It's illegal, isn't it?"

"Not for religious purposes. All you had to do was tell them you're one-eighth Koso, ask for two ounces of Peyote, and explain that it is for Church use."

"Ah," Jack said, moving over to his desk and sitting down. "I don't want to get busted attempting to buy drugs."

"It's legal!" Beck replied.

"For religious use," Jack said. "I'm not Native American. If someone has to lie about it, why don't you do it?"

Beck laughed. "Are you *serious*? I'm a freaking albino, man. Do you really think anyone is going to believe I'm part Native American?"

"Just tell them you converted. Tell them you love the Earth mother."

"That's pagan, not Native American."

"Well, then whatever they worship."

"I think you mean the Deer God."

"Meh, they're practically the same thing," Jack said with a shrug.

"See, this is why I do the thinking around here," Beck replied. Jack handed him the bag of chips. Beck took a handful and passed it back. "But I suppose it's for the best. I don't think you should be flying a two-million-dollar piece of equipment high on mescaline."

"Probably not," Jack said. They sat in silence for a few minutes. "How the hell did you even find out where to buy it?"

"I asked."

"So you just went around town asking people if they sold Peyote?"

"Pretty much. For all the good it did me."

Jack sighed, spinning the chair around.

"Do you think we'll get orders today?"

"Nope," Beck said. "It's been three weeks, and we haven't gotten anything."

"Yeah," Jack said. "What they can't do with automation, they contract out."

"I don't care," Beck said. "A few more months and we'll be done, then I can enlist another tour and plan my retirement."

Jack leaned back in the chair. "I might not do another tour."

"Why not?" Beck said. "This job is super easy."

"There's only so much time I can spend playing video games."

Beck laughed. "Not me."

"They need to let us out more," Jack said. "I feel cooped up."

"You've been back for two minutes!" Beck said. "I've been here all day."

"I mean in general," Jack said. "Four hours a month isn't enough."

"Of course, it isn't," Beck said. "How can they expect us to get in trouble with only four hours?"

The computer pinged behind Jack.

Beck sunk into his chair, fingers flipping across the keyboard. "About time," he mumbled.

"Orders?"

"Yep," Beck said. "Looks like a long run tonight."

"No video games then," Jack said. "Looks like we're going to miss our raid."

"Duty calls," Beck replied with a shrug.

Jack scanned the orders on his computer screen.

"So we're just flying around and scanning the desert?" he asked. "They aren't even going to tell us what we're scanning for?"

"Underground cave networks," Beck said.

"Your orders say that? Mine don't," Jack said. "They must love you."

He typed a few commands on his screen, then started inputting his passwords.

"Mine doesn't even tell us where we're going," Beck replied. "Just equipment readouts and prep command. They added extra equipment on this particular drone that scans ground density."

"So how will we know if we find a cave?"

"You won't know," Beck replied. "But I will."

"So I'm going to be looking at nothing except sand for the next eight hours?"

"I promise that if I see something cool, I'll tell you about it," Beck said.

"Fantastic," Jack said with a sigh. "Worst video game ever."

2

"Extension call," Beck said, his voice sleepy.

"Again?"

"Our replacement pilots aren't ready."

Jack yawned. "How long can this damn thing stay in the air?"

"Six days," Beck replied.

Jack felt his eyelids slipping closed as the images flickered in front of his eyes, showing the Middle-Eastern landscape appearing and disappearing below him. Hills, mountains, desert, plants, and repeat indefinitely.

The monitor was a blur in front of him, and he knew that he was past the limits of his endurance. He held the joystick firmly and forced his mind sharp; at least sharp enough to not crash his drone. The last thing he needed was to write a report about how he hadn't seen the ground coming.

When was the last time he'd gotten any sleep? Twenty hours ago? Thirty? He could barely remember. He had a headache throbbing behind his eyes, though whether it was from hunger or staring at his monitor too long he couldn't be sure. Only two statistics mattered to him: elevation and temperature.

They told him that those were the things he was to monitor constantly. Altitude was easy enough, just angle the plane up or down at a slight angle.

He was yet to figure out what to do if the temperature went haywire. He assumed crash.

"You know what's crazy?" Beck asked.

"What?" Jack replied, yawning.

"We are Air Force pilots. Combat operatives, protected by the Geneva Convention. But we are out here in Nevada, flying planes on the other side of the world. But, the mechanics who *fix* our drones are contracted. So, if anyone dies, it will be civilians."

"It's a new world," Jack said. "The military needs skilled labor, and it's easier to pay private companies."

"But what happens if a civilian mechanic gets caught and becomes a prisoner of war? Technically, they are civilians, but they are participating in warfare. The Geneva Convention doesn't really cover that. What happens then?"

"I don't know."

Beck was silent for a minute. "Holy shit," he said, distracted.

"What? You are surprised I don't have an answer?"

"What? No, Sorry I wasn't listening. I think we found a cave."

"Really?"

"Yeah...wait, no...maybe not. Might be an underground lake."

Jack sighed and turned his attention back to the monitor in front of him.

The clock beeped, signaling that it was after three in the afternoon.

"How much longer?" Jack asked. "And if you say another two hours I'm going to crash this thing into the next mountain I see."

"Fifteen minutes before the next swap," Beck replied.

"Those pilots had better be ready."

"Just got a ping," Beck said suddenly. He sounded wide awake. "With access codes."

"Access codes to what?"

"I'm prepping the cameras for direct satellite feed to Washington. I need to take control for a second."

"Huh," Jack said. "I didn't know you could do that."

"I didn't either," Beck said. "I'm rerouting flight control to Washington for a second."

"Important stuff, huh?"

"Looks like. Who knows, we might even get a promotion," Beck said. "Or, at least, a cookie."

Jack laughed. "I don't mind, gives me a chance to relax."

"I think we did find a cave network," Beck said. "High value. Maybe insurgents."

"Hurray," Jack mumbled sarcastically. "They better get some good pictures, then."

Beck was silent for a long moment.

"Beck?"

"They just sent new codes," Beck said. "To activate our missiles."

3

Silence held.

Neither man spoke.

"You're serious?"

"Completely," Beck replied.

"That…"

"It hasn't happened before," Beck said. Jack could hear his fingers flying as he typed in codes. "They are already picking the targets, and I'm prepping two missiles."

Jack let out a long breath. "So we're going to do this?"

"Looks like it."

"What if there are civilians?"

"In the cave?"

"There are at least people we aren't planning on bombing who will be in the way. Collateral damage."

"There usually is."

"We can't fire if there are non-combatants."

"We don't choose to fire," Beck said. "We just pull the trigger."

Jack felt a surge of anger. "Screw that."

"You're tired, Jack," Beck said. "Take a deep breath."

"I am not going to be a part of killing civilians."

"Then leave," Beck said. "I've got this."

Jack started to stand up, then changed his mind. "I'll be discharged."

"Probably."

"Because I won't kill innocents."

"Yep."

Jack sat, hands clenched on the arms of his chair, exhausted and sick with the decision. He could go to his bed, shut out the world, or he could stay and be party to the possible murder of civilians.

The screen went blank in front of him.

"Thank God," he said breathlessly.

"Son of a bitch," came the response from behind him. He heard Beck's chair spin and his headset went flying across the room. "They didn't even let us finish! Ten more minutes. That's all I needed. Ten more goddamned minutes."

"That team was supposed to take over two hours ago," Jack replied. "My brain hurts. Just let it go."

"No, screw *that*," Beck said, typing furiously.

A minute passed. The typing intensified.

"What are you doing?" Jack asked.

"I'm going to take control back," Beck said. "This was our mission."

Jack's eyes popped wide. He sat up.

"You can't."

"Like hell I can't. I'll bypass the Colonel's authorization code and reroute the drone back to our satellite uplink. I've spent all day on this mission, and I'll be damned if I'm going to let another team who wasn't even at their post get the credit."

"Beck, you can't."

"Watch me."

"Beck," Jack pleaded. "I'm not saying you *can't*. I'm saying *you* can't."

Beck paused. His fingers stopped flashing as the words sunk in. The chair spun slowly again, and this time, Jack rotated so they could face each other.

"You'll be in prison by tomorrow."

"I can reroute the IP to—"

"And I'll be in prison as well," Jack said. "For hacking and maybe for treason."

"Jack, I'm really good—"

"Are you better than *all* of them?"

This time, Beck didn't respond.

"I'm too tired to look at the screen anyway," Jack offered.

Beck sighed, accepting the olive branch. "Yeah, me too. Just frustrated. Twelve hours staring at the screen makes you kind of delirious."

"Want me to write the report?" Jack asked. Beck shook his head.

"Nah, man, I got it."

"I'm starving."

"Me too."

"Pizza?"

Beck nodded and turned back to his terminal. This time, he cleared the command screen and opened the report application.

"We still got some great stuff."

"Yeah," Jack said, agreeing to be supportive.

"And, I mean, they will still give us credit because we were on the mission, right? We set it up."

Jack hesitated for a long moment. They were going to attack something, maybe kill civilians, and maybe not. Jack hoped like hell that simply being here didn't make him accesory to that.

He said, "I'm sure they will."

4

Jack decided to burn his last hour of monthly leave and go pick up some pizza. He needed a break, a chance to cool off and think. He wanted to figure out what had just happened, and what he would have done if control hadn't been taken by the other team.

The air tasted good. Jack hesitated, breathing in the fresh air and trying to clear his headache, then walked toward the Jeep. The other trailers were closed up and silent.

Jack climbed into the Jeep and headed to the gate. He nodded at the guard on duty and held up his ID badge. The guard glanced it over, punched some data into his iPad, and handed it back to Jack.

"Last one," the guard said. "For two more weeks. You sure?"

Jack wasn't, but he nodded anyway. Right now he needed to go somewhere. He could deal with what came later, later.

He stopped outside the gate and considered his destination. He could see the lights of Las Vegas in the distance, but he didn't dare head that direction. He would never make it back to base in time, and he could get in a lot of trouble if he was caught gambling.

The appeal was there, though.

He put in an order for pizza at a local shop called Jimmie's Pizza. They thought they were Pizza Hut but with twice as much bread. Then he made his way to a gas station to pick up beer.

After a twelve-hour shift, he would fight the guards if they tried to confiscate it. He needed something to take the edge off.

He was back to base before his hour came up, showed his badge to the guards, and sighed in relief when they didn't ask to search his Jeep. He parked near the double-wide and carried the pizza and beer inside.

Beck was passed out from exhaustion, head on his keyboard and drooling. Most of the reports were sent, and he was in the middle of typing something to a general in Washington.

Jack laughed when he saw that the monitor was scrolling the letter 'k' over and over again. Beck lifted his head and looked around.

"Pizza?"

"Pepperoni and black olives."

Beck nodded, and looked at his computer: thirteen pages of the letter 'k.' With a shrug, he clicked the submit key and turned his computer off.

"Let them try to figure that one out."

"I bet the General references it in a PowerPoint this week,"

Jack said.

Beck chuckled, but now his attention was on the food Jack brought. He ripped the pizza in half and they each took a portion.

"Feels like I haven't eaten in weeks," Beck said, tearing into the food.

"The crust is too thick. And too greasy."

"This is amazing. Perfect pizza," Beck said, stuffing half a piece into his mouth. The words were garbled. They ate in silence for a few minutes. "I was checking the news earlier, and—"

"The news?" Jack interrupted. "We don't even have a TV. Our computers are part of an internal network. We can't even access the Internet without them knowing."

"What you meant to say was that *you* can't access the Internet. Don't include me in your incompetence." Beck finished off his beer and moved to grab another. "What I was going to say was, I checked the news. Nothing about a drone missile being fired, so I don't think they launched after all. Someone posted a message that drones are overused, but not big enough in social media to make me think something happened."

"For the best then," Jack said.

"That kind of thing can be career-making," Beck replied.

Jack was quiet. They finished eating the pizza and sipped on their beer.

"Want to go for a run?" Jack asked.

Beck shrugged.

"I don't really want to do anything. I'm still miffed about the mission."

"My head hurts."

"Need Tylenol?"

"Nah."

"Good, you forgot to buy some anyway."

5

The run was good. Jack took a twenty-minute shower while Beck grabbed another beer. By the time he was showered and dried off with fresh clothes, he felt significantly healthier. It was turning out to be a good day.

But the best news came when they found out they had the rest of the afternoon and next day off. The likelihood of another mission anytime soon was low.

"Guess they liked what we did," Beck said.

"I'll take it," Jack replied.

"I'm stoked. Not even sure what I want to do with myself," Jack said.

"Do you need some alone time? I can go outside."

"Ten minutes, tops."

"I think you meant two minutes."

"I've got a better idea. Let's go win some money," Beck said.

"Like poker? You want to see if some of the other pilots are up for a game?"

Beck shook his head. "Like Vegas."

Jack laughed. "Not a chance. I'm out of hours, and you couldn't even make it to the city with your hour."

"Not an hour pass. I was thinking more like a full day pass."

"They give those for family emergencies. Should I tell them my wife died? I bet that would buy me six hours."

Beck ignored him and went to his computer. "I need your login," he said.

"Why?"

"Because reasons," Beck said.

"Why?" Jack asked, but he knew the answer. "Beck..."

"Just give me the username they assigned you. I can guess the password."

"Username is JX2828CV," Jack said. "But you won't be able to crack—"

"Done," Beck said, clicking enter. The computer flipped to

40

another screen and Jack saw the normal commands flickering in front of him. "Your password is Zoe24Dillon2014."

"How...?"

Beck spun his chair around. "I'm guessing Zoe is your daughter's name, twenty-four is the age you lost your virginity, Dillon is the man you have secret sexual fantasies about, and 2014 is how many times you've watched the movie Sex and the City."

"Accurate on all accounts. Except Zoe was my first dog, twenty-four is the day of my birthday in June, Dillon is my grandfather's name, and 2014 was when I joined the Air Force. How the hell did you crack my password?"

"ESP."

"Screw you. You didn't even *try* other passwords."

"I installed a key logger a few weeks ago," Beck said with a shrug. "Don't give me that look. It's only illegal if you actually *read* the eight thousand waivers they made us sign. I wasn't planning to do anything with it. At least, not while you were here to watch me."

"You just needed to know."

"Exactly."

"Go to hell," Jack said.

Beck sighed and spun his chair around. "Rubes," he said.

He started typing commands into the keyboard, and Jack saw it flip to another screen. He couldn't read the print before it shifted to another screen, and after the next page he gave up trying.

Jack knew he should put a stop to this, even intended to stop Beck, but his intentions and actions didn't quite sync.

It was one thing to hack the pentagon and satellites and take control of a drone, and quite another to hack someone else's account and play around. Jack doubted he could do much of anything because he didn't even have admin access to anything. There might be a solitaire game he could load up.

"What are you doing?" he asked.

"I logged into your profile, then logged into an admin

account I created a couple weeks ago. It's hosted in California. I'm currently ordering you to report to Lieutenant Colonel George Orwell for a high priority mission," he said. "Don't worry, no one will ever read the report or look up the name and—"

Jack yanked Beck's chair back and stepped between him and the computer, trying to make sense of the numbers and words on the screen. Everything was shorthand and in computer terminology so he couldn't begin to understand what it meant. "Oh no—"

Beck was laughing his ass off. "It's already sent. For the next twelve hours you are the registered soldier of Lieutenant Colonel Orwell, who has listed you out on leave."

Jack felt his stomach sink.

"Damn it," Jack said, collapsing into his own chair. "I'm so screwed."

"Dude, no one reads these reports," Beck said. He slid his chair back to the keyboard and started typing more commands into the computer. "We'll be out and back by tomorrow morning, and as long as we report for duty on time in two days they won't know we left. They won't even check the admin account I made. No one would search a Lieutenant Colonel's profile without provocation."

"You aren't a Lieutenant Colonel."

"They don't know that." Beck typed for another thirty seconds and then exited out of the screen and leaned back in his chair. "There, I'm ordered out too. Now there's no way it will look suspicious since we're both reporting together."

"We're so dead," Jack said.

He felt sick to his stomach.

"Oh, lighten up. If we get caught, we'll say we went looking for this so-called Lieutenant Colonel Orwell and couldn't find him. *Someone* must have hacked the system; probably the Russians. Crazy Ruskies."

"You just hacked the Air Force control system on this base."

"Technically, I hacked the satellite relay and the California base before coming back to our system. I had to send the orders from the *outside* to the *inside*. But don't worry, that's just semantics. It's still illegal."

"If they catch us..."

"At this point, I don't care," Beck said, finality in his voice. "You don't have to come. I don't care what you do, but it's done."

Jack opened his mouth to protest and then closed it again. "If they catch us..."

"I'll say it was me. They'll know it was anyway, so you'll be in the clear, an accomplice at the most."

Jack couldn't believe he was about to say it: "We won't get caught?"

"Not a chance," Beck said. "You were right. They would have caught me in seconds with what I was planning to do earlier. They would have people tracking and scanning those connections. But this is different. Nothing can go wrong, you just have to trust me."

Jack hesitated. "Okay," he said. "I trust you."

Jack's screen flashed to life, and auto flipped to a familiar screen.

Beck clapped. "Hey! We just received orders. I wonder what they are for."

"Have I ever told you how much I hate you?" Jack asked playfully, clicking the flashing icon on the screen.

The sheet that appeared seemed legitimate, and in the orders line it said: Report to Lieutenant Colonel Orwell inside Las Vegas Immediately. At the top of the sheet was an authorization barcode for the gate.

Twelve hours.

It was the wrong choice for Jack to make. He should turn his friend in to the gate guards now before things could get any worse.

But he wouldn't. Beck was, if anything, a good friend.

Besides, it was only twelve hours. What could go wrong?

"So," Jack said, walking outside the trailer and toward their Jeep, "you any good at Craps?"

Chapter 3
Utah

1

Lyle hadn't expected it to be so hot.

Not that it was sweltering or anything here in Park City, Utah; it was just that he wasn't used to things being so arid and dry. It made him feel like he was suffocating and couldn't get enough air.

He was born and raised in Washington State where it was pretty much cloudy and rainy all the time. And humid, of course, being near an ocean. The summers got warm, sure, but it was a swampy and humid heat.

As soon as he stepped off the plane into Park City he had immediately been assaulted by the dryness of it all. It felt like his nose was going to start bleeding at any second.

He'd visited Utah as a kid, eight or nine years old; back before his father had passed away. He remembered how beautiful it was: the untamed wilderness, the mountains, and valleys stretching off into the distance, the lakes of sea salt left behind by years of evaporation.

It turned out, however, that Utah was nothing like he remembered.

As soon as he stumbled into his hotel room he turned the air conditioner on to the lowest temperature they would allow. It blasted out and he gulped in breaths of air. It tasted amazing despite having a slightly metallic smell, cooling him off and blowing his hair around. He sat on the bed, eyes closed and letting it wash over him for a good twenty minutes. He dreaded heading back outside into the oppressive sunlight where he would bake in the heat.

His cellphone started ringing. He dug through his bag until he found the little thing settled at the bottom. This was his personal cell phone, not the one supplied to him by work, which meant this wasn't a business call.

"Lyle here," he said, answering it.

"Hey, how's Utah treating you?" Peter Karnegie asked. Peter was one of Lyle's oldest friends and colleagues. He had also been his college roommate. They worked together at Markwell developing software applications.

"It's hot," Lyle admitted flatly. "No one told me it would be *this* hot."

"Yes I did," Peter said. Peter was a big guy, overweight with big rimmed glasses and fading hairline. He was pretty much always smiling and laughing, which was what Lyle liked about him. "I asked why on earth you would go to Utah for vacation."

"I thought you were being facetious."

"I wasn't. I was objecting to *anyone* going to Utah."

"You should have objected more strongly," Lyle said with a sigh. "God, I don't remember it being this hot when I was little."

"You went there with your dad, right?"

"Yeah," Lyle said. "When I was eight. We went horseback riding and hiking, and I've always wanted to go back."

"Nostalgia's a bitch."

"You're telling me," Lyle said, laughing. "My entire body is drenched in sweat and my new best friend is the air conditioner."

"You going hiking at the same places you went back then?"

"Hell no," Lyle said. "I probably won't even leave the hotel room."

"Then what are you going to do?"

"Dunno. I've got a few shows to catch up on and plenty of articles to read. I think I might learn a new language.

"I recommend Italian. The accent is sexy."

"Funny," Lyle said. "I meant computer language."

Peter laughed. "I know. Hello World. Well, enjoy the trip."

"I will," Lyle said. "It's good to be away, if nothing else."

Peter sobered up. "Yeah, I'm sure it is. How are you really?"

"Well enough," Lyle replied, lying back down on the bed. "A little freaked out still, but starting to calm down."

"I know what you mean," Peter said. "I keep expecting to get called into the office and fired."

"You think they would fire us?"

Peter hesitated. "I think if they knew that we know they would kill us," he said. "But I try to stay optimistic."

"You don't think they know, do you?"

"If they had found out then we would have heard something by now."

"Do you think we should report it?" Lyle asked.

"No one who doesn't know already would believe us, and if they know already..."

"I mean report it to higher ups."

"Like the government?"

"I don't know, maybe."

"Blow the whistle?" Peter asked.

"They have protections for that kind of stuff, right? Laws that would keep us safe."

"Not very good ones," Peter said. "If we told the right people, then best case scenario Markwell would get shut down and a lot of people would get in trouble. But, if we tell the wrong person..."

"Yeah," Lyle said. "I get it."

"I mean, I'm all for governmental oversight..."

"I get it, "Lyle repeated. "We'll just sit on the information for now. They don't know we found the back door, so there's no rush. We can decide what to do when I get back."

"Okay," Peter said. "That seems like a good enough plan for now."

"Now, if you don't mind, I'm going to get some sleep. It was a brutal flight, and I'm exhausted."

"You have to go out and experience Utah a little. Don't just spend the entire trip indoors."

"Yeah," Lyle agreed. "I know. I'll go out in a bit when

things cool off and get some dinner."

"Try one of the Pastrami Burgers. I hear they are to die for," Peter said.

"You mean like a heart attack?"

"Funny, Lyle. Real funny."

"All right," Lyle said, laughing. "Stay safe. I'll be back in a couple of days."

"You too."

"And if anything changes or someone starts asking questions, let me know."

"Believe me, if something changes, you'll be the first person I call," Peter replied. "Later."

"Later," Lyle said.

They hung up. Lyle absently tapped the phone against his chin, wondering for the millionth time just how much trouble he'd gotten himself and Peter into. He lay back on the bed, trying to calm his mind and tell himself that everything would be all right.

Chapter 4
Washington State

1

Victor waited outside the office building of Markwell, leaning against a car and tapping his fingers against the hood. It was the middle of the day, but on a weekend so there were very few cars in the parking lot. His was in a back corner, tucked out of sight.

After spending time in the Middle East, coming back stateside was hard to adapt to. It was cold and cloudy and looked like it would rain at any second. Or snow. It didn't help that he was in Bellevue in late fall.

He glanced behind him and saw Helen in the passenger seat. She was wearing a winter suit designed for the Antarctic. She was holding a worn photograph in her hand and staring at it, a slight frown on her face.

He tapped the glass, startling her. She rolled down the window.

"Stay focused," he said.

"Sorry," she replied.

"You miss her," he added, trying to get a read on Helen's emotions.

"I do," Helen said. "You don't remember anything?"

"She went in," Victor said. "We got pinned down and they bombed the building. Some debris knocked me out, and I was gone for two days. When I woke up, I heard she was gone."

Helen looked at the photo. "Yeah."

Victor couldn't tell if she believed him.

"She was a good woman," he offered.

"She was," Helen agreed, tucking the photo in a pocket. "It's going to be a whirlwind few days. You up for this?"

"Of course," Helen said.

Victor wasn't so sure. She was damn good at her job, one of the best hackers he'd ever seen, but he didn't trust her. He knew she was here with ulterior motives.

He knew no one on his team would talk to her, though, which meant she would eventually have to drop the hunt. Her sister was dead, killed by enemies in an explosion, and that was the end of the story. She might not trust him, but she was smart and knew better than to make accusations she couldn't back up. He hoped she was smart enough to just drop it.

He didn't want to have to kill her, too.

"Where is William?" he asked.

"He said he was picking up some food," Helen said. "Hamburgers, I think. Mentioned he was craving hamburgers."

Victor sighed. "Figures. Has Francis checked in yet?"

"Not yet," Helen said. "Do you think he needs backup?"

Victor shook his head. If Francis needed backup inside the building, he would radio out to them. Victor wasn't about to second-guess his second in command.

"Did you find anything out about the networks?"

"Not yet," Helen said. "I've been probing the Air Force firewalls, but I don't want to set off any red flags."

"I need you to get us inside," Victor said. "The entire job hinges on that."

"What is the job?"

"I'll tell you when the time is right," Victor said. "For now, just get us access to the networks so we can hook in. You can do that, can't you?"

"No civilians, right?"

"None," he said. "These are military targets."

"Okay."

"You can get us in, right?"

"I can," Helen said. "But their firewalls are tricky and it's going to be hard to punch a hole through without knowing more of what's inside. They don't have any easy backdoor, and I can't just try different things out with letting them know they're getting hacked. When I try to punch through, I need to do it all at once."

"How long will it take?"

"Weeks," Helen said. "I have to be gentle until I know the right places to press."

"What will speed things up?"

"I need someone who already knows the system," Helen said. "Someone on the inside."

"You know we can't kidnap anyone," Victor said. "If we hit a military base, then we're playing our hand. We will triple their security and the entire mission falls apart."

"What if we don't have to hit a military institution?" Helen asked. "What if we could just grab somebody on the outside?"

Victor frowned. "What do you know?"

"A tech reached out to me," Helen explained, "earlier this morning. Someone I used to work with who's been keeping tabs on military hackers. It looks like two drone operators went off base in Nevada with day passes."

"On leave?"

"Not scheduled," Helen said. "Things look finicky, according to the tech. I think they went AWOL."

"How?"

"Hacked the network and created false authorization. No one in the Air Force is alerted to it, and my friend found it by a stroke of luck. The General who signed them out isn't listed in the database."

"So they faked it."

"Yep," Helen said. "Which means, at least, one of them knows the system pretty damn well."

"You think we should grab them?"

"It'll speed things up and decrease our risk of triggering some internal defenses their network utilizes."

Victor thought about it for a second. "When did they go off base?"

"They've been out for about an hour, but I don't think they'll stay overnight. They have twelve-hour passes. If I had to guess I'd say maybe seven, eight more hours before they head back inside."

"All right. I'll have a jet prepped. Figure out which casinos they are hitting and find us a place to grab them."

Helen nodded. "You got it."

"You're sure it's worth it?"

"It could save us weeks of probing," Helen replied.

"Then make it happen," he said.

The door to the office building opened up. Francis stepped outside, carrying a laptop under his arm. As soon as Victor saw his face he knew something was wrong.

"What is it?" he asked once Francis was close.

"We've got a problem."

"What? Did you get the package?"

"I did," Francis said, "but our contact told me someone figured it out. They were snooping in the code and found the backdoor."

"Who?"

"A couple of developers. Nobodies."

"Did they report it to Markwell?"

"No," Francis said. "The contact only found out this morning when he saw a trigger in the logs. He wants to know what we want him to do."

Victor turned to Helen. "What about the government? Anything recent on the web about this?"

She was typing frantically on her computer, searching for any trace of a leak. After a second she looked up at them. "No word. Yet. No one is talking about software vulnerabilities with Markwell"

"So it looks like they kept their mouths shut," Victor said.

"Looks like," Francis agreed.

"Still loose ends," Victor mused. "Who are they?"

"Peter Karnegie and Lyle Goldman. Mid-level developers."

"Both local?"

"Yes," Francis said. "But that's the other problem. Lyle is out of town on vacation."

"When did he leave?"

"This morning. He went to Utah, and his plane just touched down a few hours ago."

"Perfect," Victor said, scratching his chin.

"You think it'll work?"

"Like a charm," Victor replied. "Have the contact plant something inside to make it look legit, and you can put something on his friend. Make it look like a sale went wrong."

Helen looked between them, a confused expression on her face. "What?"

Francis gave her an irritated look and turned back to Victor. "Africa?"

"Iran," Victor said. "It'll hit the news faster."

"I'll make sure the contact gets the story straight."

"What are you guys talking about?" Helen interrupted.

Victor sighed.

"Here's what happened," he explained. "Lyle killed his friend and stole the software his company develops. He was planning to sell it to Iran."

"Peter is dead?"

Victor smiled slightly. "Not yet."

Helen looked like she'd eaten a rotten piece of fruit. "So you're going to frame Lyle and make it look like he stole the software?"

Victor nodded. "And when no one knows where Lyle disappeared to they'll focus all efforts on finding him. We won't even be on their radar."

"He won't be that hard to find," Helen said. "We found him in like two minutes."

"When you drop a body into a pigpen they eat everything," Victor said. "Even the bones and teeth."

The look on Helen's face was abject horror. She was trying to hide it but doing a poor job of it. Victor almost laughed, she looked so pathetic.

He would need to keep an eye on her. Make sure she didn't do anything stupid.

He looked to Francis. "Take care of Peter and the contact."

"You got it," Francis replied, handing Helen the laptop from Markwell and disappearing down the street. He tucked his hands in his pocket, bracing against the cold.

Victor turned to Helen. "We're going to Nevada to pick up your pilots. I'll call and have a local team take care of Lyle. Go find William. We're leaving."

2

Peter stepped into the foyer of his home and shut the door, rubbing his arms. It was cold, and he'd forgotten his big jacket when he ran to the store.

It had taken three different stops before he finally found pastrami but now that he had a half pound of it, he could already taste his sandwich. Some slices of Gouda cheese to top it off, along with an immodest helping of mayonnaise. He headed into the kitchen, opening the bag and taking out his sliced deliciousness.

Maybe he should toast the bread first and then put a slab of butter on it before layering the pastrami—

He froze, halfway into the kitchen in midstride. The hairs went up on the back of his neck: something was wrong.

"You should have reported it," a voice said from his living room.

The house lights were still off, but he could dimly see a shadowy figure standing in the doorway. It was a small man, lithe with dark hair. He had a thick British accent.

"Who...why...?"

"If you *had* told someone, then this would have been a lot harder for me. We would have needed a new plan and killing you could have been a liability. It might have been enough of an inconvenience to just scrap our entire job and let you live."

The man stepped forward, flicking on the kitchen light.

"Now, however, it's just unfortunate that you sat on the information."

"You...you shouldn't be here," Peter said, feeling his knees wobble. He could barely breathe, and the words were little more than a whisper.

The man smiled at him. "I shouldn't be a lot of things. What is the password to your computer?"

"Wha...what?"

"Your computer," the man repeated. "I have to put a few documents on it, and it's best if I don't break my way in. I want them to look as legitimate as possible instead of a log of failed password attempts."

Peter gulped. "Are you going to kill me?"

"Yes."

Peter dropped his bag on the floor.

"The question is: am I going to have to torture you first?"

Peter turned and ran for the door. He made it two steps before the man was on him. He felt a stinging pain in his back, followed by agony ripping through his body as the knife jerked up. Before he could scream a hand covered his mouth. He tried to pull it away, but the grip was like iron.

"The password," the man whispered in his ear. "And this is over. Try to scream and it will last all night."

Peter whimpered.

"You understand?" the man asked. Peter nodded feeling tears in his eyes from the pain and fear. The man's hand disappeared. "What is the password?"

Peter gave it to him.

"See? That wasn't very hard," the man said. "I'm a man of my word."

He felt the blade draw back ever so slightly and then it suddenly twisted. Peter's knees buckled and he screamed, but the hand was back, clamped on his mouth. He screamed into the hand, feeling agony and dizziness wash over him. The world turned red and became pain.

"Mostly."

Chapter 5
Las Vegas

1

"Which Casino do you want to hit next?" Beck asked as they found their way back to the main thoroughfare. Jack shrugged, pleasantly tipsy and enjoying the atmosphere. The lights, the music, the action. He felt like dancing, like months of excess stress were being scraped away.

"We already hit Caesar's and Paris. How about we check out the Mandalay this time?"

"I was thinking Excalibur."

"Seriously? It's disgusting."

"I've never been there."

"I went four years ago with my uncle. It's dingy," Jack said. "But we can go there if you want."

"Well, how about the MGM then?"

"Sure, that one is good."

They headed outside to the Jeep. Their first stop had been to pick up new clothes, something to help them blend into the Vegas landscape. Beck was wearing jeans, a long sleeve T-shirt, and sunglasses, trying to cover as much of his albino skin as possible.

Jack elected for a polo shirt and dress pants, tucking his wallet into the front pocket.

Jack climbed into the driver side of the Jeep and rolled down the window. It was a hot and muggy afternoon, and he was already starting to sweat. Jack noticed something in Beck's hand as the albino buckled himself in and burst out laughing.

"Condoms?"

"You know," Beck said, blushing, "just in case."

"Are there a lot of girls there interested in a shiny guy?"

"Oh, screw you," Beck said, blushing deeper. "And I got extra, in case you need some. But you'll have to settle for Regular. They didn't have any extra small."

Jack stopped laughing. "No way, man. That's one line I won't cross. I'm married."

"Okay, okay. I was just throwing it out there. Tonight, I'm getting laid."

They headed into the MGM and split up. Jack found himself at a Black Jack table some time later, debating whether a queen-six pair was worth hitting.

Two people already busted, and he tried to think back to exactly which cards were played in the game so far. He liked to think he was good at math and probability, but he knew that he wasn't smart enough to exploit a casino.

Sixty percent chance he would bust? Thirty? How many cards were even in the dealer's deck at this point? Jack couldn't even think of a good number to *make up* as the probability, let alone do the real math in his head. Instead, he decided to trust his intuition and called for a hit.

Bust.

He sighed, stood up from the table, and went hunting for Beck. The casino was huge with a vaulted ceiling. The buzz and whistle of machines surrounded him. He had a Samuel Adams that was starting to feel warm, so he quickly drained it and tossed the bottle into a trash can.

It had been four hours, he was down three-hundred fifty dollars and drunk enough that he didn't care. He needed to find Beck because if there was anyone who would understand the probabilities of card games, it would be his math- wizard friend. Jack spotted him near a slot machine and maneuvered through the crowd.

"I'm up six hundred," Beck said when he noticed Jack. "Enough for a decent hooker."

"Or six crappy ones," Jack offered. He watched Beck for a minute. "I'm down."

"How much?"

"I don't want to talk about it," Jack replied. "Let's just say you're loaning me money for dinner."

"Four hours left before we need to head back. I'm thinking we can get a lobster dinner sometime soon, then hit a few more casinos," Beck said. He reached to the side and grabbed a martini.

"Is that an Apple-tini?" Jack asked as Beck took a sip.

"Watermelon."

"Seriously?"

"Don't judge me," Beck said, then drank the rest of the martini and set the glass aside.

"And you wonder why you can't get laid."

Beck ignored him. "Two more spins and we can go get food."

"I want to try one more hand of Black Jack; I'm feeling lucky. Speaking of which, do you know how to cheat at Black Jack?"

"It isn't cheating. Just math."

"So you know?"

"It's not that hard, just takes time and patience. Do you have a memory palace?"

"A what?"

"A memory palace. Something you remember really well that you can associate to the cards? For me, it's my home. I imagine walking into the foyer, and then I see the coatrack and think of the Jack of Hearts and then the cabinet where my mom stored her knitting supplies and think of the queen of diamonds. As I move through the house, I place other cards alongside things I remember so I know what cards have already been used."

Jack was silent for a long moment, wobbling slightly in his drunken daze. "What's a foyer?"

Beck sighed. "Never mind."

"Uh huh. I'd rather just get dealt a Black Jack. That sounds easier."

"The likelihood of being dealt a Black Jack is five percent, whilst the likelihood of being dealt a hand that is hard standing is thirty percent. That means the likelihood of being dealt a hand where you have to make a decision is around forty percent. The trick is to wait until the chances skew in your favor and then put your money down."

"Did they teach you that when you joined the military? I must have been stuck in the shitty boot camp," Jack said. He felt like giggling. He didn't though.

"I learned it in video games."

Jack chuckled and took a sip of his drink, leaning against the slot machine. "You done yet? I'm starving."

"I thought you wanted to play another hand of Black Jack?"

Jack shook his head. "I can't afford to lose any more money."

"All right, I'm going to take a piss, then we'll hit the restaurant."

Beck stumbled out of his chair and weaved his way through the crowd to the restroom. Jack watched him and couldn't help but chuckle.

"Drunken bastard," he mumbled.

"Who?" a voice asked behind him. Jack almost fell down he was so caught off guard. He stumbled into the machine and banged his shoulder before catching his balance.

"Sorry, ow," he said, rubbing his shoulder.

"I didn't mean to startle you," a young woman said, stepping back with an amused smile on her face. She was gorgeous, just over five feet tall with brunette hair.

"I...uh...do I know you?" Jack asked.

She shook her head. "No, but you were leaning on the slot machine I was hoping to use. Your friend just won a few hundred dollars on that machine, and in my experience its best to borrow someone else's good luck when I run out of my own. Maybe I can steal some of his."

Embarrassed, Jack stumbled aside so she would have access to the machine. She smiled at him and sat down, slipping a few dollars into the machine and pulling the lever. Jack decided to walk away and wait for Beck near the bar, then he could flag him down when he came out of the restroom and they could go eat.

Except, even after making the decision, he didn't move. Jack watched her play the slots, paying more attention to her than the machine, as she lost a few pulls. He wanted to walk away, to push her out of his memory, but he couldn't.

She was angular and beautiful, and he was drunk which made her look like a super model. It was more than four months since he'd seen his wife in person, and he suddenly couldn't stop thinking about her and how much he missed her.

"Superstition never pans out," the girl said, punching the machine and shrugging at Jack. "Forgive me for being rude. I was just hoping that one of these days I would actually win money here."

"No apology necessary. I'm just waiting for my friend," Jack replied. "I'm Jack."

"Helen," she said. "From Jersey. My girlfriends brought me here for my birthday. I'm in a sorority. Alpha Phi Omega!" She threw her hands up and laughed. "Are you from around here?"

"Yes," he said. "Actually no. I'm sort of from this area...for now...but I live in Arizona and...never mind, it's complicated. For the sake of argument, I'll say yes, I live near Vegas."

"Well, Jack from Las Vegas," Helen said sweetly, "would you be so kind as to pull this lever for me after I put a dollar in? Maybe I can borrow some of *your* luck."

"I've been losing all day, so I don't think that's a good plan," he said, stepping forward to pull the lever. She slipped a dollar into the machine.

They won, and the machine went wild with pinging noises and music. She cheered and slipped another dollar in, gesturing for him to work the lever again. He won again, though a smaller amount, and sat down next to her to get a better angle on the machine.

"Looks like you are lucky."

"Do I get a part of the spoils?" he asked. She smiled and leaned close, whispering into his ear, "No way, but I'll think of a consolation prize."

2

"Sorry, I uh...shouldn't...can't...uh...won't," Jack said, shaking his head. He cleared his throat. "I'm married."

"Oh," Helen said, pouting. "That's too bad."

"I love my wife," he said.

"She's a lucky woman," Helen replied, frowning.

They sat there awkwardly and then Jack climbed out of the chair. "So uh...I'm just going to go find my friend."

"Hang on just one more second," Helen said, pulling out her phone. She started tapping on it, not looking at Jack. "You know, it's actually kind of endearing. Victor thought you would come with me without question."

"Uh...what...?" Jack asked, feeling his body tense up.

"He said if I wore the same perfume your wife wears and look cute you would do anything I asked. I thought maybe you would be a good guy and not cheat on your wife, so I came with a backup plan."

Jack blinked and took a step back.

"What is going on?"

"We already have Beck. I spiked his drink, so when he got to the bathroom they had no trouble leading him upstairs. That should be enough to convince you I'm serious, but just in case..."

She pulled a little dart gun out of her purse and shot Jack with it. Then she slipped it back in her purse. Jack jerked the dart out of his chest, instantly feeling woozy.

"What...what shoot...shot with me?" he mumbled, mind unable to focus on anything.

"A very mild sedative, which when mixed with all the alcohol you consumed is going to make you very sleepy."

He yawned. "Why did that you?"

Jack staggered into the machine. Several people turned to look, and a man in a tuxedo came over to see what was wrong.

"My husband has had little too much to drink," she said, smiling at the man.

"Shot..." Jack tried to explain. "Shots, she shot..."

The man smiled understandingly at Jack. "Would you like help to get him upstairs?"

"Oh, would you?" she asked. "That would be most kind. I think it would be best that he sleep this off."

"Of course," the man said, grabbing Jack under the arm. They started toward the elevator.

"I..." Jack said helplessly to the man as they rode upstairs. "Shot."

"Yes," the man agreed. "I love their shots as well."

"No, no," Jack argued. "She...I...shot..."

The elevator dinged at the floor, and Jack felt himself dragged along. He was panicky but too tired to really feel the effects. All he wanted to do was go to sleep.

They were in front of a door. The woman slid it open. "Thank you so much."

"Do you need any help?" the man asked.

"I think I can get it from here," she said, grabbing Jack under the arm. "There you are, honey."

She got him in the room and closed the door. She dragged him over to the bed and dropped him face first into the sheets.

"I've got him," she added.

And then Jack passed out.

Chapter 6
Utah

1

Lyle finally decided it was late enough to vacate his hotel room.

He'd spent most of the day lounging, and it was getting into the early afternoon. He'd read a few articles about recent advances in the field of robotics, watched some TV, and now he was starving. It had been several hours since he had last eaten.

The sun hadn't set yet, but the day had cooled off significantly. A quick check of his phone told him that the heat was only in the lower eighties. He looked up some nearby restaurants and settled on a hole in the wall diner a few blocks away.

He hadn't rented a car, so he would be hoofing it across the city or taking taxis. He decided to walk to the place and ride a taxi back because he doubted he would want to walk after he'd eaten, and he didn't want to waste too much money getting driven around.

The walk wasn't too bad and he found the weather to be quite enjoyable now that it was cooler. He nodded pleasantly at a few people along his way and enjoyed the fact that there were very few clouds in the sky. It was nothing like Washington. Maybe he would stay up late tonight and find a place to do some stargazing.

"Welcome," a hostess said as Lyle entered the restaurant. "How many?"

"Just one," Lyle said.

"For now? Is the rest of your party on the way or is it just you?"

"Just me," Lyle said with a sigh. The hostess looked

puzzled like she couldn't understand why he would come to the diner alone.

"All right," she said. "You can follow me."

She put a handful of menus back and led Lyle through the restaurant to a table in the corner. It had four chairs, and Lyle picked the one closest to the door.

"Thanks."

"Your server will be right with you," she replied, disappearing.

Lyle pulled out his phone and started scrolling, not really searching for anything in particular but wanting something to do to pass the time. He texted Peter a quick message about an article he'd read earlier and then checked his Facebook account.

"Hi," a teenage kid said, stepping up the Lyle's table with a notepad in his hand. "I'm Fred, and I'll be taking care of you. Can I get you started off with something to drink while we wait for the rest of your party to arrive?"

"It's just me," Lyle said.

"For now?"

"Nope," he replied, "and I'll take a Coke."

"Sure," the kid said, flipping his notepad closed and heading back into the kitchen.

Lyle sighed and put his phone away. His stomach was rumbling as he glanced over the menu, trying to decide what he wanted.

Suddenly, a woman sat down in the chair across from him. She was holding a menu up, hiding most of her face. "You should try the bison burger," she said, not looking at him. "It's out of this world."

Lyle looked around. "Excuse me."

She lowered the menu and smiled at him. "Yes?"

He opened his mouth, trying to think of something to say. "This...uh...is my table."

"I know," she agreed, looking back at the menu.

The waiter reappeared with a Coke. "Ah, okay, you're all

here now?" he asked.

"Yes," she said.

"No," Lyle said.

"What would you like to drink?"

"I'll have the same thing he's having," she said.

"She's not with..." Lyle started to say, but the waiter was already walking away, completely ignoring him.

"You didn't get diet, did you?" she asked.

"What?"

"I hate to diet. It gives me headaches. That fake sugar is disgusting."

"Who are you? Do I know you?"

"Nope," she admitted, lifting the menu. "How about we split a bison burger? It's pretty big, and I don't think I can finish the entire thing."

"Who are...why...um...what are you doing at my table?"

She stared at him. "Eating."

"I mean, why this table?"

"Because there are empty chairs."

"But, I mean, wouldn't you prefer..." he trailed off.

"If you have something to say, just say it," she said.

He took a deep breath. "This is my table, and I don't know you. I would prefer if you went somewhere else."

"There, that wasn't so hard, was it?"

She looked back at the menu. Lyle waited for a second, then said, "So, are you going to move?"

"No, but I appreciate that you said it."

The waiter reappeared. "Did you guys decide what you want?"

"We're going to split the bison burger," she ordered, handing him the menu. The waiter took Lyle's as well. "To go. And there's an extra twenty in it if you can get it in the next three minutes."

The waiter looked surprised for a second and then shrugged. "Sure."

He disappeared back into the kitchen.

"Why are you doing this?" Lyle asked.

"Because I'm hungry," she replied, "and I don't know when we're going to be able to eat next."

"What are you talking about?"

"Can I see your phone?"

"No, you can't see my phone," he said.

She gave him a look that made the hairs on the back of his neck stand up. A shiver ran up his spine.

"Why do you need my phone?" he asked.

"Because they will use it to trace you," she said.

"Who?"

"The FBI when they realize you're a traitor. JanCorp when they realize you're still alive. Take your pick."

"What?"

"Just give me your damn phone."

Lyle thought to object, but it was hard to figure out what was going on. "This is a joke, isn't it?" he asked. Nevertheless, he handed his phone over.

She flipped it over, took off the back plate, and removed the battery. Then she put both pieces into her pocket.

"Might need it later," she said.

"Did Peter put you up to this?"

She took a sip of Coke, not looking at him. "Peter's dead."

Lyle hesitated. "What?"

"They killed him about an hour ago in his home. Made it look like you did it."

"No, no, that's impossible. I just talked to him."

"I need to know why," she said. "Why do they want you dead?"

The waiter reappeared with a bag. He handed it to the woman. "Here you go."

"Thanks." She handed him two twenties. "If anyone asks, we were never here."

"All right," the waiter said. He looked confused but just disappeared into the kitchen.

The woman stood up. "We're out of time, but as soon as

this is over, you need to tell me everything. Got it?"

"What are you talking about?"

She looked at the front of the restaurant. "Start walking back to your hotel. Act like nothing is wrong. Don't look around when they start following you."

Lyle shook his head, unable to think straight or figure out what was happening. "What is going on?"

She leaned in close. "Hey," she said, grabbing his chin. "There are too many civilians in here. Children. They wanted to grab you in here, but I convinced them to get you outside first. If you don't start walking in the next ten seconds, then a lot of people are going to die. You don't want that, do you?"

Lyle just stared at her, feeling his heart beating furiously in his chest. Without saying anything, he stood from his chair and started walking for the exit.

"Take this," she said, handing him the bag of food. "And don't drop it. Like I said, it might be a while before we get to eat again."

2

Lyle walked down the street, fighting the urge to look around. His legs felt like rubber and he was lightheaded, like he might pass out at any moment.

Just a prank, he told himself. Some stupid prank that Peter is playing on me.

He just wished he could believe it.

The first block went smoothly as he walked down the sidewalk. It was getting dark out and with it came a chill in the air. He wasn't hungry anymore; his stomach was twisted in knots.

The street was almost empty, with only a few people walking in either direction. He crossed to the second block and saw a black unmarked van pull up to the curb in front of him. It was about fifty feet away, idling.

He let out a gasp of air, trying not to fall over. His body

was tense and he felt wobbly, but he kept putting one foot in front of the other.

He heard footsteps behind him, closing the distance as he got closer to the van. "Oh God," he muttered. "Oh God, oh God, oh God…"

The footsteps behind him sped up just as the door to the van swung open. Suddenly, he felt something slide over his head and the world went dark. A bag. He was pushed forward, and he tripped. Someone caught him, and he felt himself dragged up into the van.

He was blubbering and thrashing, but strong arms held him down. He heard the van door slide closed and they started moving. Lyle could feel the van underneath him jostling as they traveled.

He kept muttering to himself, biting back the urge to cry and trying not to panic. "We've got the package," he heard someone say.

"An easy grab," another voice said. This one he recognized as the woman from the diner. The one who had sat and spoken with him.

"What's this?"

"Looks like his leftovers," another voice said.

The first man laughed. "He won't be needing those."

They drove for a while, jostling and laughing and pinning Lyle to the ground. It was hard to breathe, and he felt lightheaded. His entire body was shaking.

"Why are you doing this?" Lyle asked. His voice was muffled.

"Shut up," one said, hitting him on the side of the head.

"This far enough?"

"Yeah, pull up here out of sight. We'll drop him in the trees."

The van pulled to a stop but kept idling.

"Grab the shovels," the first person said.

There was the sound of rustling and then the van door slid open. Lyle was dragged out, panting into his bag.

"Please, you don't want to do this!"

They ignored him. The person dragging him threw him roughly forward to the ground.

"Start digging the hole. We'll put him in first."

"Please..." Lyle muttered, trying to crawl away. Someone stepped on his leg.

"Going somewhere?"

A few laughed. Suddenly, there was the soft *pssh* sound of expelled air.

"Hey, what—!"

Another *pssh*, then another. Someone started shouting, and Lyle heard scrambling around him. A body thudded to the ground a few feet from him and he jerked away from it.

There was a scuffle with a lot of thuds as people punched and hit each other, then another *pssh* and then silence. Lyle could hear his own breathing, sucking the cloth bag into his mouth then blowing it out, always short of breath. It was quiet outside his bag, and he felt his body trembling in fear.

The bag was yanked off his head. He drew in air, gasping. Four bodies lay on the ground around him, scattered and in various positions. All of them were unconscious.

The woman from the diner stood overtop him, holding what looked like a long-barreled pistol. She had a bloody lip and looked slightly disoriented.

"Get up," she said, offering him a hand.

He tentatively accepted it, and she jerked him to his feet. He dusted himself off and gulped.

"What...what happened...?"

"I shot them," she said.

He stared blankly at her. "Are they...?"

"Tranquilizers," she added, shaking her head. "They'll wake up in a few hours with raging headaches, but otherwise, they'll be fine. Except him—" she kicked the boot of the nearest guy—"I had to break his arm."

"You...you helped them take me."

"Of course I did," she said. "That's what they hired me for.

And I needed the van and a place to stash them while we figure out what to do next, so I let them bring us out here."

"They were going to kill me."

"Yep." She walked over to the van and reached inside. She pulled out the bag of food from the diner. "You dropped this, but I grabbed it."

"Oh."

She opened the bag and pulled out the sandwich. She ripped it in half and offered him a piece. "Eat."

"I'm not hungry."

"Yes, you are. Eat and you'll feel better."

Just thinking about the food made Lyle nauseuos. "I don't think I can right now."

"Either eat this damn sandwich or I'll shoot you."

Lyle took the offered half. He bit into it, but he couldn't taste anything. He chewed mechanically and swallowed.

"Why were they going to kill me?"

"You tell me."

"I have no idea," Lyle said. "I'm nobody."

"Not to them," she said, taking a bite of the sandwich and grabbing some fries. "You were worth a five-person hit squad."

Lyle rubbed his chin and then staggered over to a tree and leaned against it. "I...have to sit down."

"It's okay. Deep breaths. The adrenaline will wear off and the weakness will pass. What do you know that is worth getting you killed?"

"Nothing," he said.

"It already got Peter killed."

Lyle felt a tightness in his chest. "God..."

"We don't have all day."

Lyle looked up at her. He dropped the sandwich on the ground and felt like he was about to cry. "It was all a mistake," he said.

"What was?"

"When we found it."

"Found what? Start at the beginning."

Lyle took a deep breath. "We were doing performance testing and I wanted to shave a few seconds off of one of our worst performing services. It was an application we weren't supposed to touch and the code was obfuscated, but I started playing with it to find out where I could save some time."

"Obfuscated?"

"Means intentionally confusing. Like they wanted to make it transparent."

"Transparent?" she asked. "Like see-through?"

"What? No. The coding meaning of it. Like, completely predictable but hidden from the user."

"Oh," she said. "So you were messing with stuff you shouldn't have been?"

"No one told us not to mess with it," Lyle said, "they just figured if they made it confusing enough we wouldn't bother. Anyway, it wasn't an issue until we found the backdoor."

"The what?"

"Whoever originally built the software added some clever weaknesses. External access that is almost impossible to use unless you know exactly what you're looking for. But, with it, you can gain complete control of the system."

"Why would they do that?"

"To let someone in who isn't allowed to be there," Lyle said.

"Like who?"

Lyle shrugged. "China. Russia. Anyone who knows about the weakness can exploit it."

The woman was silent for a second. "How many devices would this affect?"

"Thousands of drones all around the world. Many are military but some aren't."

"So with this exploit, someone could take control of a drone and fly it wherever they wanted to?"

"You're missing the point," Lyle said. "With this software, someone could take control of a drone and bomb a city."

3

The woman was silent for a long minute. "Damn."

"Yeah," he said.

"And now they know that *you* know?"

"There must have been some protection on it. When I checked out the files in VC it probably pinged whoever created the exploit."

"VC?"

"Version control," Lyle answered.

"Can you start talking like a normal person?"

He lifted his hands helplessly.

"Sorry about your friend," Kate said.

Lyle felt like crying again. The idea that he would never see Peter again was impossible to comprehend and unfathomably sad at the same time. "Peter was a good guy. And I got him killed."

"Don't think like that," she said. "Everyone makes their own choices."

"I told him to download the software."

"You didn't know it was an international security risk."

He sighed. "What now? Do I report this to the government?"

"Won't do any good," Kate said. "Get up, we need to go."

"What do you mean it won't do any good?" he asked, standing up.

"The people who killed Peter framed you for it, and they planted evidence both in the company and at Peter's house that you are a spy stealing the software. As far as the FBI knows, you've been planning to sell it for a while to Iran. Peter was on to you, so you killed him to keep him quiet."

"What? That's ridiculous."

"Not to the FBI," she said. "There's going to be a manhunt for you in the next few hours, so we need to get you out of the state."

"And go where?"

"East," she said. "I need to get you out of sight and get us to a position where we can figure out who really took the software and what they are planning to do with it. Then we can stop them."

"Why?" he asked. "Why are you helping me?"

She opened the door to the van, finishing the last bite of her sandwich. "I have my reasons," Kate said.

"How do you know so much about what's going on?"

She glanced over at him. "The people that are doing this…I used to work for them."

Chapter 7
Unknown Location

1

Jack awoke groggily, opening his eyes in the dim lighting of his holding cell. He was on a hard-backed bed with almost no padding. His head hurt, and he felt as though he'd been decked in the temple.

He was in a rundown holding cell; less than a ten-by-ten cube without windows. Dust covered everything, and it looked as though it hadn't been used in many years.

A flickering fluorescent light glowed above him and the only furniture was a toilet in the corner and the bed he was residing on. The toilet was also made out of steel. There was, at least, running water.

He thought back to the night before, piecing together the details of his capture. He tried to figure out what they might want from him. First, he remembered being in the casino, then he was approached by a young woman who had taken him captive.

But, the question he couldn't answer was: why him? Why kidnap *him*? What did he know that they would need?

He remembered her mentioning Beck, which made him even more certain that this wasn't a random happenstance. They knew what they were doing.

But...what were they doing?

2

More importantly, what had happened to Beck? They walked into this trap together but was Beck all right? Jack hoped they hadn't done anything to his friend.

Jack stood and walked to the bars.

"Hello?" he asked. "Is anyone there?"

There was no reply. He waited at the door for a few minutes and walked back to the bed.

His headache only got worse as he sat there, worrying and frantic. They had snuck out while on active duty after Beck hacked the system, and now he was sitting in a jail cell that hadn't been used in a long time. He couldn't imagine things being any worse.

He was sitting on the lumpy bed when the door opened. The young woman from the night before walked in, smiling and calm.

"Hi, Jack, glad to see you finally awake."

He didn't reply right away, trying to get his raging emotions under control. He felt anger at her for what she had done to him, but it was masked behind several layers of fear and confusion. She was out of the skimpy dress now, wearing simple and loose fitting clothes. Her hair was disheveled, and she had bags under her eyes.

"What do you want?"

"I heard you were a fantastic chef, and we were hoping to steal your recipe for chocolate truffles," she replied. She waited for a second and then laughed. "No, not even a chuckle? I thought the reason was obvious."

"I'm a drone pilot," he said.

"Bingo," she replied, pointing her finger at him like a gun. "You're a lot smarter when you aren't drunk."

He hesitated. "I'm an Air Force pilot, and they will be looking for me. You don't..."

He trailed off when she started laughing.

"You are a *drone* pilot. They probably won't even notice you are missing for a few weeks. Worse, you left of your own accord, so even if they were looking for you, it's to charge you with a crime and then discharge you."

Jack couldn't think of a good reply to that.

She bowed. "My name *really* is Helen. I wasn't lying to

you."

"What do you want?"

"What does anyone want?"

"I'm not interested in idle chit-chat," Jack said. "So tell me what the hell you want or get out."

"Touchy," she said, making a tsk sound at him. "I see you don't want to be friends, so I suppose I'll get down to business. You helped hack the satellite relay that runs your drone software, and we need you to do it again."

Jack was about to tell her that he had no idea what she was talking about, then realized he did. He started laughing, and she turned crimson.

"What's so funny?" she asked.

"You think I hacked something? I can barely turn my computer *on*. I can't help you."

"Bullshit," Helen replied, narrowing her eyes. "Your login was used to bypass the security systems. You and Beck hacked into the security network."

"Beck used my login," he said. "But I sure as hell didn't hack anything."

3

Helen was annoyed.

The office they were in was an old police station. JanCorp used it as a safe house for various operations. Most city plans actually assumed it was demolished or decayed, but it was maintained throughout the years and gradually forgotten.

"We didn't need both."

"I thought we would," Victor replied with a shrug.

"You had me dress up like a doll to trick this asshole, and he isn't even useful to us."

Victor tapped his chin. "You did look pretty nice in that dress."

"Screw off."

Victor ignored her, tapping his chin.

"So what do we do with Jack now?" she asked. "Let him go?"

"Not yet," Victor said. "Not until after we're done with Beck."

"It's just an extra mouth to feed."

"Then don't feed him."

Helen was silent for a second, trying to decide if that was a joke or not.

"Why do you think Beck used his login?"

"What?"

"Was he using Jack as a patsy?"

Helen shrugged. "I don't think so. My guess is if Beck was a good enough hacker he might think people are watching him and his logins. They wouldn't be watching Jack, so using that login would have been a simple security decision."

"So you don't think he was intending to betray Jack?"

"I doubt it," Helen said.

"Good," Victor said, standing up, "then Jack might have some use still yet."

Chapter 8
Arizona

1

Kate sat on the edge of the bed, pondering her next move. They were hiding out in a hotel off an exit ramp outside Phoenix. A little remote exit well out of the way. She had booked it early that morning and been careful to keep her face off any of the cameras.

It was close to a few major highways, which meant as soon as they figured out where to go they could be on the road. That was important because she wasn't sure how long it would take to get drones in the air once the software was compromised.

She'd burnt most of her bridges saving Lyle from the hit team and didn't have a lot of contacts willing to help.

She'd hoped to grab the pilots too, to keep them out of Victor's hands, but it was too far away and she hadn't found out about them until the last minute. After talking to Lyle, they were the last piece of the puzzle Victor needed to put together before he had control over the grid network of almost thirty thousand drones.

Unfortunately, no one in JanCorp that she still trusted knew where the pilots were being held. Somewhere in Arizona was their best guess. That left too many stones to turn until she could narrow things down. She didn't know exactly where she should look next.

She was starting to wonder if saving Lyle had been worth the effort.

Lyle was lying on the other bed, staring up at the ceiling.

"What are you thinking about?"

"Hmm?" he replied.

"I asked what you were thinking about."

He sat up. "Nothing, really."

"Nothing at all?"

"My life was just ruined. I'm a fugitive from the law. A huge part of me thinks that I should turn myself in right now."

"I can't let you do that."

"I know. And you scare the hell out of me, so I'm not going to do anything stupid."

"Plus, I'm trying to help you clear your name."

"Are you?" he said. "That's the thing I've been wracking my brain to figure out. Are you really trying to help me or is there something else to this? I don't even know you."

"I'm Kate."

"Sure," he said. "But I don't know if that's even your real name."

"It is."

"Why would I trust you?"

"I saved your life."

"Doesn't make you an honest person," Lyle argued. "It means you need my help."

"Not necessarily," she said.

"Then why? Why seek me out?"

"Because you have value."

"I'm wanted by the FBI."

"For something you didn't do."

"They don't know that."

"Are we just going to argue all day?"

"Maybe," he said, lying back on the bed. "Is there anything else to do?"

Kate sighed. "No. Not yet. We need more information."

"How are we going to get more information?" Lyle said. "I can't exactly ask a lot of questions without tipping off the FBI."

"No, you can't."

"I can't believe…" Lyle muttered, trailing off.

"Can't believe what?"

"I can't believe they would sell me out like this. After everything I've done for them."

"You built their security network?"

"In a sense," he said. "I took all of the tools they are using and wired them together. A few pieces were customized, and I helped write a few really important algorithms. But, I mean, why me?"

"Why not?"

"What?"

"You helped build this software of which reputation is everything. And that reputation is built on its security. What happens when it gets hacked?"

"Huh? It isn't *supposed* to get hacked."

"Humor me. Let's say someone at Markwell knew the software was going to get hacked because it already knew about the backdoor. If people do hack it, what do they do with it?"

He shrugged. "Bad things, I suppose."

"Big bad things," she said. "Like front page news bad things."

"Yeah," he agreed. "Depending on what they do with the software."

"And, when front page news bad things happen, somebody is going to take the fall. You worked on this software, which means you serve two purposes for them. First, they get someone to blame for this catastrophe. Everyone points their finger at you, and no one realizes just what really happened."

"And what's the second thing?"

"They get you out of the picture and you aren't a risk anymore."

"They'll kill me to keep me from talking?"

"You know things they don't want anyone to know. Killing you isn't a far stretch."

"I'm starting to think..."

He trailed off. There was a buzzing sound suddenly, coming from the bed. Kate tensed, turning to Lyle.

"What is that?"

"What is what?"

It buzzed again. It sounded like...

"Is that a phone?"

He reached into his jacket pocket and pulled out a cell phone. It buzzed in his hand.

"Oh..." Lyle said. Kate turned to stare at him with a mixture of incredulity and shock. "Oh yeah. About that..."

"You have two phones?" she asked, snatching it from him.

"It's a work phone. I never use it."

All thoughts of her plan were out the window, and she felt a little sick to her stomach as fear filled her. "Why didn't you say anything?"

"I forgot about it."

"You forgot that you had two phones?"

"There were some other things on my mind at the time," he said. "Sorry."

"Sorry? You think *sorry* is going to cut it?"

"What are you mad at me for? I thought you were the super spy."

Kate rushed to the window and glanced outside. Several police cars sat in the parking lot, along with a swat vehicle. None of them had their lights on, but she knew what they were here for.

"Could this get any worse...?"

There was a banging sound on the door. "Police. Open up."

2

Lyle was terrified. Kate walked over to him and leaned close to whisper. "They don't know you're here, only the phone."

"They can turn on the microphone and listen."

"It will take a few hours to get a court order for that. For now, they just have GPS and are sweeping the building. Get in the closet."

"Why?"

Another knock on the door. "Open up."

Kate pushed Lyle back toward the closet and locked him

inside, then slid the phone into her purse.

She mussed up her hair and pulled the sheets loose on the bed, and said "I'm coming, I'm coming," with a Brooklyn accent. She opened the door, yawning.

Two police officers stood there. "Ma'am," one said.

"What do you want?" she asked.

"We need to search your room."

"Why?"

"We have reason to believe a fugitive wanted by the FBI is hiding out in this hotel, and we are searching every room."

"Okay. How long is this going to take? I was trying to get some sleep. Long flight, you know?"

"It won't take long."

She stepped out of the way to let them in. "Okay, but be quick about it."

They came into the room and began looking around. She waited until their backs were turned before drawing her gun. They looked under the bed and checked the curtains.

"Are you here alone?" one officer asked. Neither was looking at her.

She closed the door and fired off two quick darts. Both hit the necks of the officers and they slumped to the floor. Kate opened the closet.

Lyle saw the two cops on the ground. "What happened to them?"

"Horse tranquilizers," she said, taking out Lyle's cell phone and sliding it between the two officers. "When they don't report in, the swat team will be sent to check it out."

"What happens then?"

"By then we will be long gone," she said. "But first, we need their uniforms. Strip them."

Lyle stared at her. "What?"

"Take their clothes off. It's going to be a little big for me but should fit you nicely."

Lyle didn't reply, but with a sigh he started taking the unconscious officers' clothes off. Kate put on the first officer's clothing overtop her own and took both of the Tazers. She waited until Lyle was dressed and then handed him one.

"We aren't killing anyone," she explained. "That would put us from the category 'nuisance' to 'cop-killers.' But knocking them out, that just pisses them off."

"Will these disguises work?"

"Not for long, but enough to get us out of the building. The swat team is going to be coming up the north stairwell, so we're going to go there and wait until they get sent in. Then, we just slip out behind them, find a car, and disappear."

"What if they recognize me?"

"Good point," she agreed.

She opened her microfiber travel bag and pulled out a small container of makeup. She turned to face Lyle.

"You're kidding, right?" Lyle asked.

"I'm only going to use a little bit," she said. "Kneel down and close your eyes."

Lyle looked around, let out a long sigh, and knelt in front of her.

She opened the small case and lifted out the brush. "Close your eyes and turn your chin up," she said. "No, more like this. Now tilt your head so it's level."

"This is so emasculating," Lyle said, closing his eyes. Kate held the brush up as though she was about to apply the makeup. She waved a hand in front of his eyes to make sure he wasn't peeking and silently pulled the makeup back. "I just want you to know that I think this is a bad plan and if—"

Kate stood up and kicked Lyle in the face as hard as she could, hitting him with the flat top of her foot on the left cheekbone below his eye. His head jerked to the side, and he collapsed to the floor.

Lyle was looking around delirious, almost blacked out, and she couldn't suppress a giggle.

"What the...?" Lyle asked breathlessly, trying to get his bearings. His left eye was closing and the right was twitching wildly.

"That's for carrying two phones," she said.

"Did you have to punch me so hard?" he asked, trying to sit up.

"With your cheekbone bruised your face will swell up and turn blue. It will distort your facial proportions and make it hard for anyone to recognize you, even with facial recognition software," she explained. "And now you don't have to use makeup. Aren't you happy?"

"No," he said. "I'm sure as hell not happy."

"Fantastic," she said.

Kate looked him over and saw that his face was already swelling up and changing color. Maybe she hadn't needed to kick him *that* hard.

Oh well, nothing she could do about it now.

At least, she felt better.

"Let's go."

Chapter 9
Arizona

1

Lyle could barely breathe while they walked down the stairs. Kate seemed calm and relaxed, not at all bothered by what they were doing. Once they reached the bottom floor of the stairwell, they hid around the corner and waited.

"What now?" he asked.

"Now," she said, "the swat team will come in and we will slip out."

"How long does that take?"

"Depends on how efficient they are," she said. "They were probably supposed to check in after clearing each floor, but it could have been each room. I'd say another few minutes at most."

Turned out to be ten minutes, and it felt like an eternity to Lyle. He kept shifting, feeling lightheaded and dizzy. Kate had kicked him hard in the face and it was throbbing.

When the door finally sprang open he almost cried out. Five men in swat uniforms came in, carrying assault rifles, and started up the stairs. They didn't notice the two fugitives hiding around the corner.

Kate waited until they were a few flights up and then headed toward the door. "Just stay calm and follow me."

Lyle followed, barely daring to breathe. Once they were outside, they saw swarms of people looking at the building, mostly civilians but with officers and detectives mixed in.

Kate walked confidently along the building. No one paid them more than a passing glance. A few saw Lyle's bruised eye and stared longer, but no one seemed to recognize him.

They made it through the crowd, and Kate directed him

toward the back lot of cars. As soon as they were hidden behind some brush she stripped the officer's clothes off. She found an open car and tossed the shirt inside, then the pants. Lyle did the same.

Then they found another unlocked car and climbed in. "Do you know how to hotwire it?" he asked.

"Of course," she said, popping it open and playing with the wires.

"What if someone comes by and asks what we're doing?"

"Then stall."

"Stall? How am I supposed to do that?"

"I don't know, show them a magic trick."

Lyle sighed. It only took Kate a few seconds to get the car turned on and moving. They drove slowly out of the parking lot, using a back exit that hadn't been closed off. Once they were on the road heading away from the hotel Lyle started breathing easier.

"That sucked," he said.

"Yes it did," she agreed. "But you didn't do too badly considering."

"You kidding? I couldn't even think straight."

"But you didn't freak out," Kate said. "So maybe there is hope for you yet."

"My face hurts."

"Sorry about that."

"No you aren't," Lyle said.

She shrugged. "No, not really."

"Where are we going now?"

"Farther east," she replied. "By all reports, that's where Victor is holding up."

"Who's Victor?" Lyle asked.

"He's the guy running this entire operation," Kate said.

"You used to know him?"

Kate was silent for a long moment. Finally, she said, "No. I don't think I ever really knew him at all."

Chapter 10
Unknown Location

1

Beck couldn't think of any good ways out of his predicament. After being drugged and kidnapped, he'd been locked into a chamber behind a one-way mirror in an old police station. No one had come to speak with him and he'd been left with a two-gallon container of water, some dry foodstuffs, and a bucket.

They had grabbed him in the bathroom, but he hadn't been able to put up much of a fight. He had a raging headache and felt exhausted, probably from the alcohol. He didn't drink much, but he remembered downing several drinks at the casino.

One of the guys who grabbed him was massive, at least, three hundred pounds of muscle. Beck didn't think he would be able to fight his way free: the guy could snap him like a twig.

Finally, after what felt like a decade alone in the cell, the door opened. A small man walked in, thin and well built.

They stared at each other for a long minute before the man spoke. He had a thick cockney accent and spoke slowly.

"We have you in a secure location. No one knows where you are."

Beck thought of a snarky response but changed his mind. "Okay."

"I want you to understand how dangerous this is for you. If you refuse to help us, we will resort to violence."

"Help you how?"

"You're going to show us how to hack into the drone networks."

Beck mulled the words over. "No."

"No?"

"No, I won't do it."

"I don't think you understand how—"

"I do," Beck said. "But you're asking me to show you how to perform a terrorist act."

"You've done it before."

"But never with bad intentions," Beck said. "I do stupid things all the time, but never to hurt other people. *You* plan to hurt people. So, no, I won't help."

The man looked at him, sizing him up. Beck thought he would speak again, but instead, the man left, leaving him alone in the room once more.

2

Francis walked through the halls of the old Peoria police department; the walls were whitewashed, bare, and faded, with more than half of them converted to canvases by graffiti artists.

He found Victor in an old office, leaning against the desk and looking up details on his phone.

"He's being difficult," Francis said, stepping inside and closing the door.

"Won't help?"

"Not willingly."

"Fix it."

"I will," Francis said.

Victor looked up at him. "Fix it now."

"I will," he replied smoothly. "But that isn't what's bothering you."

"Our deadline is being moved up."

"Why?"

"They are doing construction on the school," Victor replied.

Francis processed the information. "So the children will be home."

"Yes."

"That was never part of the plan."

"It is now," Victor said. "They will pay triple."

"Then it's about the money?"

"This is about sending a message."

"To who?" Francis asked.

Victor hesitated. "Our job is to deliver the message."

"If Helen finds out…"

"You think I care what Helen does or doesn't find out?" Victor said. "She's not even on my radar."

"She will try to sabotage us if she knows," Francis said.

"Then don't let her know," Victor said.

"She isn't dumb."

"No," Victor said. "She's too alike with her sister."

"Want me to take care of it?"

"After," Victor said. "We still need her until she gets into the network."

"Then we need her to work with Beck," Francis said. "So we need to break him."

"He pretends he doesn't care about anything, but he does. Everyone has something they will die for; it's just a trick of finding where to apply pressure."

Victor turned to face Francis, and the look in his eye sent a shiver down Francis's spine.

"Maybe Helen was right about which man we need, after all."

Victor walked down the hall, leaving Francis alone. After a moment, Francis followed, but when Victor went into the room with Beck, he went into the other room to watch through the one-way mirror.

Victor strode in, ignoring Beck and walking to the table. He sat down and gestured for his captive to sit across from him.

Victor drew a nine-inch blade from a hidden sheath inside his pant leg. He gently laid it on the table in front of him and sat down. He met eyes with Beck but said nothing.

A minute passed, then two, and still Victor waited in

silence. Finally, Beck couldn't resist the silence anymore.

"What's that for? So you can cut off my fingers? No, you wouldn't do that. I need those to type. Maybe my toes. That's more reasonable."

Beck tried to act tough, but his voice was high pitched and squeaky. His bravado wouldn't hold. Victor didn't reply, but continued to stare and wait. Another minute passed, and Francis could see Beck getting more and more uncomfortable.

"I won't help you kill people," Beck said.

"We aren't asking you to kill anyone," Victor replied.

"But you're asking me to give you a weapon that *will* kill people. It's the same thing."

Silence again.

"We will kill your family," Victor said finally, "but that won't do any good. You don't respect them. You no longer love them. You've been apart for too long."

"I will mourn them," Steven replied. "But since I'm not killing them I won't feel guilty."

"You would be causing their deaths."

"I would," Steven said. "But in doing so it would prevent other deaths."

"The people I am asking you to kill are ones you've never met," Victor said.

"At least now you are admitting that *I'm* killing people."

Victor ignored him. "They are people you would never meet under normal circumstances. If you help me, I will let you live. I will let your family live. There will be no repercussions. People will die, but you will not be personally responsible.

"If on the other hand, you refuse to cooperate, I will kill Jack Wallis," Victor continued. The response from Steven was surprise, but well-disguised. "But not until after I kill his entire family. His daughter will be first. I will tell his wife it was Jack's failure as a man, husband, and friend.

"His wife, I will beat, forcing you and Jack to watch as she pleads for it to stop. Only after she has declared that he failed her and their family will I tie him to the ground, hang her body in the air, and slice her throat. He will watch the life leave the eyes of the woman he cherishes, and I will leave him there until she begins to rot. Then I will release him, covered with his wife's blood, so that he can find the most suitable way to end his own life."

Victor sat silently, hands folded on the table in front of him.

"I will do all of this because of you, and I will make sure he knows it was *your* fault. You will be the cause of his family's suffering and death."

Beck was speechless.

"This is the knife I will use," Victor said, holding it up to the light.

Beck's lip was trembling. "Why are you doing this?"

"That isn't your concern."

"Who..." Beck started to say, then let out a shuddering breath. "Who do you plan to attack?"

"A military target," Victor said. "No civilians will be harmed."

"You swear it?"

"I do," Victor said. "I will be the one killing enemy combatants. Not you. The only way you will kill anyone is by doing nothing."

Victor stood, slid the knife away, and disappeared back into the hallway. Francis waited for a second and then Victor came into his room. They stood side by side and watched through the window.

Beck was practically shaking in his seat. All of his bravado was gone. His tough guy attitude had been silenced and he looked like a broken young man.

After another minute or so, Beck slid his chair back and walked over to the glass window. Staring at the ground, he whispered, "I'll do it."

Chapter 11
Arizona

1

Kate sat at the desk in their second hotel room, tapping her fingers against her chin and staring out the window. This one was on the first floor and she was determined to keep a better eye on what was happening outside.

Now that they knew Lyle was in the area they would start combing the area, and she wanted to be able to drop out of sight if they came to check out this hotel.

"This room has a kitchen," Lyle said. He was lying on the bed next to the air conditioner. He had it blasting on full, making the room cold.

"The oven doesn't work," she replied.

He sat up. "That's an oven? I thought it was a dishwasher."

"Why would they have a dishwasher in here?"

"Why do they have an oven?" Lyle asked.

"In case you want to cook something."

"But it doesn't work."

"You just have to lift the top off to work the burners and...never mind," she said.

"Even the mini-fridge isn't cold," Lyle said, lying back down on the bed and crossing his hands over his stomach. "What's the world coming to when hotel rooms include a fake kitchen just for ascetics?"

Kate didn't have an answer. They sat in silence for a few more minutes.

"Your face looks terrible."

"Oh does it?" Lyle said, touching his swollen cheek. It was black and blue now, and puffy. "It hurts like hell."

"Especially when someone reminds you of it, right?"

He looked up at her, frowning. "You aren't a nice person, are you?"

"Not really," she said with a shrug.

"So what's your interest in this?"

"Huh?" Kate asked.

"Why are you involved?"

"Why do you want to know?"

"Because I think it's personal for you," Lyle said. "I think you don't really like what's happening, but you especially don't like Victor. What did he do to you?"

"It's complicated."

"A past lover?"

She laughed. "Not a chance. Do I detect a hint of jealousy?"

"From me? No way," Lyle said.

"Mmhmm."

"So, what's the story?"

Kate was silent for a moment. "I don't tell the story."

"Why not?"

"Because it's personal, and I don't give out personal details."

"You know everything about me," Lyle said. "Why can't you tell me something about you?"

"Because you are a mark," she said.

The words came out harsh, a lot meaner than she'd intended, and she instantly regretted it. In the reflection from the window, she could see Lyle's hurt expression.

"Oh," he said, lying back on the bed.

Kate opened her mouth to apologize and then hesitated. Finally, she spoke. "Look I'm sorry—"

"No, it's fine," Lyle said flatly. She could hear the hurt in his voice. "You saved my life because you need my help. So what do you need help with?"

"Figuring out who they will attack."

"If you let me use your laptop, I can get into my employer's system and start fiddling around."

"It's too dangerous," she said. "By now your login

credentials are compromised and if you try anything they'll track you here."

"I wasn't planning on logging in," Lyle said. "I know how to use the backdoor."

Kate thought about it for a second.

"Okay," she conceded. "Try to find a way in and look around for any information that might be useful. Do you need any help?"

"No," he said.

She bit her lip and sighed. "All right. I'm going to go take a shower."

"Okay," Lyle said. She started walking toward the bathroom. "Hang on."

"What?" she asked.

"Those two drone pilots they picked up earlier," Lyle said, typing. "One has family that doesn't live too far from here."

Kate froze. "I thought they lived in Florida."

"They moved a few months ago," Lyle said. "You don't think they might want to use them for leverage, do you?"

Kate hurried to the door, cursing the bad luck. "Stay here."

She doubted she would make it in time.

2

Kate found herself driving alone down the interstate, frustrated that she'd missed the Intel about Jack's family. She'd been so off-guard and unprepared for this entire situation that she was being sloppy. Normally, she wouldn't have missed something like this.

Of course, she'd entirely missed Victor trying to kill her.

Which was why she wasn't behaving normally. In previous jobs with a client or asset similar to Lyle, she would tie him up in the bathroom or on a chair in the room and leave him until she was done with whatever she had to take care of. There was no way she would trust him, let alone give him her computer and possibly get them both caught.

And, why the hell did it bother her that she'd hurt his feelings?

She sighed as she pulled into the driveway where Jack's family lived. The house was quiet and empty, and she knew she was too late. The back door was closed but showed the telltale marks of a crowbar where someone jimmied it open.

There were signs of a scuffle inside where the wife had fought back, but they had subdued her quickly. Upstairs, Kate found empty bedrooms but saw nothing useful.

More than a little frustrated with herself, Kate picked up the house phone, dialed 911, and left it off the hook. She slipped back outside, careful to make sure none of the neighbors saw her.

Safely in her rental and on the freeway again, she relaxed. She felt her phone start vibrating.

"Anything yet?" she asked.

"I know who the mole is," Lyle said. "One of the VP's. I got into his email, and he's been talking to some people. They are vague, but I know they are talking about the backdoor."

"Okay," she said.

"He references a warehouse in Arizona in one email. I'm trying to track it down and I'll let you know as soon as I figure out how it relates. Did you find Jack's family?"

"Gone."

"Damn," Lyle replied. "Do you think…do you think they'll be okay?"

Kate didn't have a good answer. "I hope so. I'll be back in half an hour."

"All right. I should have the warehouse location by then."

3

Beck sat at the terminal beside Helen. He was running a skeleton project that was similar to the network she wanted to hack to show her how the connections worked. She was incredibly smart, picking up on the small details a lot faster than he had expected.

"All of the security services use two way bit stream connections, but we need to override the internal framework to allow it to transmit and receive simultaneously."

"So they built it with extra overhead?"

"It's bad design," Beck agreed, "because it means we can hide our own commands in output functions."

"Wow," Helen said, leaning forward to see better, "I could never have found that."

"With a built-in lag period, by the time we communicate with the network, it already sent out our fake override code. Then we can embed a new admin into the system and log in through it."

"And once we are on their network, we can bridge the connection to Markwell's software servers and run all the relays from there," Helen said. "That's perfect."

"Don't get ahead of yourself," Beck said. "I've looked at Markwell's network, and it's way more sophisticated. We can't brute force our way inside."

"We already have that taken care of," Helen replied.

"Oh?" Beck said. "You have a backdoor in the code?"

She nodded. There wasn't any point in lying.

They sat for a minute, looking at the computer. Suddenly, Beck said, "Why are you doing this?"

"Doing what?"

"This," he said, gesturing toward the computer. "You don't seem like...the others. Why are *you* a part of this?"

Helen hesitated. "I have my reasons."

"What reason could you possibly have that justifies killing innocent people?"

"We are attacking a military base," Helen said. "No innocents."

"You honestly believe that?"

A moment passed. "No," she said. "I suppose I don't. But I don't have much choice."

"No," Beck said. "*I* don't have much choice. You have all

the choice you could want. Just leave."

"I can't," she replied.

"Why not?"

"I just can't," Helen reiterated. He could tell he was hitting a nerve. She wasn't a killer.

"What are you going to do with Jack?"

"Let him go," she said, "after we finish the job."

"What about me?"

"Probably let you go as well," she said. "You won't serve any purpose once we're done."

"Probably," he echoed. "Can you, at least, tell me what's going on? What are you actually doing?"

She didn't respond. She got up and headed out of the room, leaving Beck alone. He thought maybe he'd pushed her too far and annoyed her too much, but after a few minutes, she came back. She had Jack with her, and he looked just as confused as Beck did.

Beck ran over and gave Jack a hug. "I'm sorry, man. I'm so sorry."

"It's fine," Jack said. "It's not your fault."

Beck turned to Helen. "What's going on?"

"Victor is still out. William and Francis are watching the exits."

"Okay," Beck said, confused. "What does that mean?"

"It's in Texas," she added. "The target is a little town called Cottonwood Heights."

"Why there?" Beck asked.

"I don't know," she said. "Victor told me it was a military installation, but I don't believe him."

Jack let out a sigh. "Why are you telling us?"

"Because I don't know what is going to happen to you two, and if either of you are able to escape I want you to warn them."

4

"Why don't you just let us go?" Jack asked.

"I can't," Helen replied, "because they have your family. If I let you go, they'll hunt you down, kill your family and then kill me."

"My family? Are they okay?"

"They are fine," Helen said. "And they will remain fine as long as Beck keeps helping."

Jack looked at Beck. "Don't worry," Beck said. "I would never do anything to jeopardize your family."

"Why are they doing this?" Jack asked.

"I don't know," Helen said. "Look, this is the best I can do. Hurry up and say your goodbyes to each other because I need to get Jack back in his cell before they know something is up."

Jack gave Beck another hug and then followed Helen down the hall. "Why are you helping us?" he asked.

She was silent, then gestured for him to head into the cell. Jack did, and she locked it.

"Because I know how important family is."

Chapter 12
Unknown Location

1

Jack waited in his cell, repeating the name of the city in his mind over and over and trying to relax. Helen had risked a lot getting the information to both of them, and he was determined that if he could escape he would put it to good use.

The only problem was: escape didn't seem remotely possible. At least not under his current circumstances. Helen had moved him back into his holding cell almost twenty minutes ago after letting him see Beck. It was nice knowing his friend was alive and well.

After about half an hour of waiting, the door to his cell opened and a giant man walked inside. Three hundred pounds of muscle. The man stared at him for a second, then gestured for him to get up.

"Time to go."

"Where?" Jack asked.

"Another location. Get up," the man replied. Jack stood from the bed and waited for the man to back out of the small cell. "We're going to visit your family."

Jack felt his heart skip a beat. His family. His worst fear brought to light. He'd been praying they wouldn't know about his family or at least would leave them out of this.

"What do you mean?"

"What do you think I mean?"

"Are they safe?"

"For now. But they might die. Too soon to tell. If your friend stops helping, then they will die for sure."

Jack winced.

The man led him through the dimly lit police station into

an alleyway. A black truck was waiting. The cab was enormous, but he still doubted that the man felt comfortable inside. His head must touch the ceiling.

The giant man opened the passenger door and handed Jack an empty black cloth bag.

"Put that on."

Jack stared at it for a second, then looked back to the truck. The wheels sat high and the floor of the front cab was around his waist. "Can I climb in first? I don't think I'll make it if I'm blind."

The man narrowed his eyes, then stepped out of the way so Jack could climb in. He lifted himself into the cab and the door shut behind him.

He saw that the keys were in the ignition. The giant was walking around to the other side of the truck, oblivious. Jack could slide across the seat and start the truck: gun the engine, lock the doors, and escape before the man caught on.

Then he could get his bearings of this city, find help, and let people know what was going on.

But he didn't slide across the seat. Too many things could go wrong. The huge man might be armed, and a lucky shot could end the escape in seconds. Plus, Jack didn't know where his family was being held and didn't want to risk their safety.

He put the hood over his head and waited. A few seconds later, the driver's side door opened and he felt the truck shift under the man's enormous weight. The truck started and he felt it lurch out of the alley. With an internal groan, he kept repeating the name in his head.

2

Victor paced the doorway of the warehouse, eyes on the infant girl he held in his arms but mind far away. Things were progressing nicely and he was only days away from finishing the mission. It was nearing midnight, and he was expecting William to arrive at any moment.

That was part of the reason he was holding Jack's daughter right now. The emotional effect would be instant, lending credibility to the statement he was going to make. Marian Wallis, Jack's wife of three years, was crying softly from behind, but that didn't bother him. She was worried for her daughter, Jack was worried for his family, and Victor was worried about his job. Everyone had something at stake.

"Your father will be here soon, and you can go home to a nice warm crib," Victor said softly to the baby, gently tapping her nose with his finger. The sobbing intensified behind him, and he heard Marian whisper, "Please…"

"Your daughter is fine. As long as things go smoothly you will be home in a few days," Victor said.

Marian was tied to a chair in the doorway of the warehouse, framed nicely in the dim light to make her glow. All seven of the guards posted at this safe house were out of sight at the moment, two patrolling the exterior and the other five guarding the interior.

It was packed with hundreds of enormous crates. Some were supplies, some weapons, and a lot were old and abandoned goods left behind by the original owners of the warehouse. Rotten foodstuffs and moth-ridden clothing.

Victor had decided to move Jack to the location because he didn't need him anymore, but he also didn't want to let him go. He'd pulled a few local guards on JanCorp's payroll to look after Jack and his family until the mission was over and then they would cut him loose.

Now that things were progressing smoothly, he had no doubt he would be able to lock everything down in time for his morning attack. He would send his message and then he would tie up all of the loose ends.

Including Helen.

"Please let us go," Marian said softly. Victor stopped pacing and faced her.

"If you want to have an intelligent conversation, I will gladly participate. But if the only thing you can manage is a half-assed plea for help, keep your mouth shut. The last thing I want is for Jack to show up and find me beating his wife for her incessant nagging."

The double shipping door to the warehouse began grinding open and he stepped out of the way. A large black truck drove to the edge of the warehouse entrance and parked.

The passenger door flew open, and he watched Jack stumble out of the truck. The pilot ran across the pavement to his wife, kneeling next to her and throwing his arms around her. Victor didn't intervene, standing to the side and waiting.

"Are you okay?" Jack asked, almost crying. She stammered something, but Victor made out the words. She was delirious and terrified. "Thank God you're safe."

After thirty or so seconds Jack stood up and glanced around. His eyes locked on his infant daughter in Victor's arms, and he took a step forward.

"She's fine," Victor said. "She has your nose."

"I'll kill you if you hurt her," Jack said, his voice soft.

"I have no intention of hurting you," Victor said. "Or your family. Not if you don't do anything to us."

"We won't say a word," Jack said. "We'll do whatever you want."

Victor smiled and handed him his daughter.

"Then our business is concluded," Victor said. "Play nicely, and you'll get to go home."

Then Victor got in the truck with William and they started to drive off.

"We aren't going to kill him?" William asked.

"He's military," Victor said. "If we kill him, they'll hunt for us. If we let him walk, then when they find him they will charge him for his crimes. He'll be too busy dealing with his own problems to worry about us."

3

Jack knelt beside his wife in the warehouse with his daughter in his arms. The truck was gone and they were alone, and he was rocking his daughter. She'd stopped crying and was sleeping, but he doubted it would be long before she was crying again. He looked at his wife and saw that she was crying as well.

He felt horrible; this was his fault. If he'd never disobeyed and gone into Vegas this wouldn't have been possible. And now his family was suffering because of him.

How selfish was he that he couldn't survive a few months of boredom? His eyes started welling up and he knew he was going to cry soon too if he didn't find something to occupy his mind.

"Jack, what's happening?" Marian whispered.

He hesitated. "I'm sorry. I'm so sorry about everything. I don't know what's going on. But I promise you we'll make it out of this okay."

"No, we won't," Marian replied. "We won't."

"Don't say that. We'll be fine. They promised to let us go if things work out for them. We'll make it out of this."

She was still shaking her head. Jack shifted around to behind the chair and adjusted Jessica so her head was on his shoulder. With a free hand, he worked on the bonds, trying to free Marian's hands. It was difficult and slow, but after a few minutes, he managed to finagle the ties enough that she could work her hands free.

Triumphant, he leaned back from the chair and saw that there was a guard ten feet away watching him. So much for small favors. A heavy machine gun hung at the man's shoulder and he seemed more amused than anything else.

"Don't mind me," the guard said. "I'm just here to shoot you if you run."

Jack ignored him and finished getting Marian's hands free. She rubbed her wrists.

"Better?" he asked. She nodded, sniveling, and reached out for her daughter.

Jack handed his daughter over and stood up, positioning

his body between his family and the guard.

"Jack, they are going to kill us," Marian whispered, brushing the thin strands of hair out of their daughter's face and rocking her.

"No, they won't," Jack said. He wished his voice was stronger, wanted desperately to encourage her that everything would be okay. He wanted to mean it. Unfortunately, he didn't believe it. "They won't hurt us."

Not yet at least. Not until they've killed Beck.

4

"Are you done?"

"It's not as easy as it looks," Lyle said. His fingers bounced rapidly over the keys, flipping through pages faster than Kate could keep up with.

"Give me an idea. Are you, at least, close?"

"I'm on the state's network and I found applicable buildings."

Kate waited, but Lyle didn't say anything else.

"And...?"

"And that means I'm on their network. I have access to their systems, but I'm not completely sure what I'm looking for."

"Safe house locations."

"There isn't a file conveniently labeled 'hey dummy, here's the data you're looking for.' I found a lot of GPS coordinates, but I'm trying to isolate which ones are currently being used and which have been abandoned or are owned by shell companies."

"What do you mean? Just find abandoned ones in Arizona."

"There are six-thousand-four-hundred-and-fifty of them."

Kate blinked. "What?"

"Yeah, so if you'll be quiet for a few minutes, I'll try to figure out which ones are active, and of those which are likely to be used for hiding people in remote locations."

Kate sighed and kept pacing the hotel room. A few minutes dragged past before Lyle spoke again.

"Found one," he said. "It's a warehouse outside the city. It's been closed, and they have it flagged for demolition from seven years ago. It's an hour away."

"Okay," she said. She picked up her pistols. "Let's go."

Lyle shrunk away. "What do you mean 'let's'?"

"We need to leave now."

"What do you mean 'we'?"

"You're coming with me."

"Why on Earth would I do that?"

"Because I might need backup."

"Then call in some backup."

"From who? I don't have anyone. And I don't have time to call in any favors, so you're the only backup I've got."

"Then in that case," Lyle said, closing the laptop, "we're screwed."

5

Lyle had to pee.

Or at least, his body was doing a convincing job of creating the symptoms. He'd tried five minutes earlier and nothing came out, so he knew it was just nervousness. That didn't change the fact of how he felt, though, and he wanted desperately to find a tree to duck behind and relieve himself.

He was leaning against the side of a warehouse next to Kate. She was peering around the edge and scanning the front of another building two hundred feet from their position.

He wasn't sure exactly what she was hoping to see, but it was taking a long time. And each time he tried to look around the edge she gently pushed him back. So he'd given up and was staring out into the desert of Arizona instead, wishing there were more trees.

Or at least, a big cactus nearby. But there was nothing

except empty desert in front of him. They were on the outskirts of the city, watching the warehouse he had flagged and waiting.

"Anything?" he asked finally.

"Nope. No movement."

"Maybe we're at the wrong place," he offered. "I could have picked the wrong one."

"No movement is a good thing. This is supposed to be an abandoned building, so if there were a lot of people milling about outside I'd be worried." There was another long pause, and she heard a faint sound. A second later, she heard and engine start, then fade away: "A side door just opened and someone left."

"What's the plan?"

"It's not much of a plan, but here's what I was thinking," she said, looking at Lyle. The grin on her face made him realize she was about to make fun of him. "You charge straight at the front door, screaming like a maniac. When they open it to shoot you, wet yourself and curl into a fetal position."

"How does that help?"

"They'll never shoot someone covered in their own urine."

"Uh..."

"Then, I want you to start crying and crawl away. In the meantime, I'll sneak through the back, rescue Jack's family, kill the bad guys, and meet you at the car."

Lyle shrugged. "You know, I actually think I might have that in me. No one screams like I do. I'm not really digging the charge forward part, though."

Kate only sighed.

"I'm serious. What the hell am I doing here?'

"You've fired a gun before, right? Just pretend it's target practice."

"Targets don't shoot back."

"Don't over think it, just react. When the fight starts, let go of your inhibitions."

Lyle nodded. "Yeah, that's about the time I expect to start

wetting myself."

"Shut up and follow me," Kate said, reaching down to the device clipped to her belt and flicking a button.

Lyle saw her eyes light up, as though they were reflecting a glare, but there was nothing casting light nearby. She hesitated. "Why are you looking at me like that?'

"What was that?"

"Night vision contact lenses."

"That is the coolest thing I've ever seen. Can I have a pair?"

"Maybe when you're older," she said, glancing around the side of the cactus.

Lyle closed his eyes, took a deep breath to steady his nerves, and opened them again, ready as he would ever be.

"Okay, let's do this."

Kate was already gone.

6

Kate sprinted forward and ducked behind a car, putting her back against the wheel and readying her pistol. The nearest patrolling guard was less than two hundred feet away, and he would pass by less than twenty feet away within moments.

Once he was gone, she would have forty seconds to get inside the warehouse before the next guard patrolled past. She was expecting it to be locked, so she was ready with a pick. That was plan A. She also had a sizable chunk of plastic explosive in her pocket with a detonator at the ready as her backup plan.

She felt a thud against the car next to her and winced. "You could have told me we were moving—"

Kate reached forward and put her hand over his mouth. He stopped talking and stared at her. Fifteen seconds later and they heard footsteps. His eyes widened, then closed tightly.

She shifted to see underneath the car and watched boots pass them. She waited until they were around the corner of the warehouse and took her hand off Lyle's mouth.

She did a quick scan of the area and sprinted to the side door. Locked. She knelt down to work the tumblers.

"I didn't even see him," Lyle said, coming up next to her and panting. "Holy crap."

"Shut up," she said, "and get ready."

"And do what?"

"Make sure no one sneaks up behind me."

"You know if you go to Home Depot and buy all the doorknobs and keep a key from each package you can open almost any door? Most locks are universal, and the only ones you can't open that way are custom made. That's like five percent of all doors."

"Oh my God, do you ever shut up?"

"I can't help it. I'm terrified."

"Most people talk less when they are terrified."

"I can't help that I'm not like most people, and by now I would think you would understand that this is not something normal people do, and I'm starting to freak out—"

"Just watch my back," she said, working the last tumbler into position.

She felt it click and gently turned the handle. She cracked the door and peered inside. It was dark, but not excessively so. A high walkway ran through the center and connected free hanging offices.

It was packed pretty thick with old crates and there were walkways running above it in dozens of directions. To her right was a stairway leading up, and she decided that would be her first destination.

She expected guards to be on walkways so they had the best vantage possible, and it wouldn't be advisable to move through the interior without understanding its pathways. The rail would be a good starting point.

"Follow at a distance and stay ready," she whispered.

"Got it."

"And whatever you do, don't get shot," she said.

Before Lyle could respond Kate was gone. She stayed crouched and moved to the stairs, rifle at the ready.

The only strong light source was at the enormous front door. She figured Ben would either be there or in one of the offices at the opposite end of the hanging walkway. She slid around the edge of the stairs and crawled up, slinging her rifle over her shoulder.

The stairs were made of grated aluminum with handrails and no sides, so anyone glancing her way wouldn't have much trouble spotting her. She moved as quickly as she dared to the top and peered over.

At the opposite end of the warehouse were the offices, and about halfway down the walkway it split off to the right and left, leading to other staircases heading down. At the split stood a guard, scanning the interior, and another was positioned in front of the enclosed offices. That was a good sign.

At least, there was something worth protecting in there. She searched around, hoping to spot any other guards, but it was too dark and cramped on the ground floor. She did a quick recap in her mind: two patrolling outside, two on the walkway, and at least one near the light source at the front shipping doors of the warehouse.

Kate forced her mind clear and slid the rifle off her back. With a flip of her finger, the laser beam shot out, aimed at the stairs for now. It was an ultraviolet laser, invisible without a filter. She could see it perfectly, but with luck, no one else would be able to.

She took a deep breath, held it, and lined up her first victim. The dart whistled out of the gun with only a small expel of air. It hit the guard in the arm, knocking him unconscious before he could cry out.

He fell face first and rolled off the side of the walkway. He thudded noisily into the boxes below and Kate cursed under her breath.

"So much for keeping this quiet."

Someone shouted from farther in the building. Kate lined up the second shot and released two more darts at another guard. He collapsed against the door behind him and slid to a sitting position, unconscious.

She quick-stepped up the stairway and lined the rifle over the edge. She spotted a third guard running for cover. Kate fired another dart and he fell in mid-stride, hitting the ground with a hard thud. If he hadn't broken his nose, Kate would be amazed.

The response to her attack came faster than anticipated. A bullet hit the aluminum by her hip, and she dropped to her back, sliding down a few stairs as more bullets clanged around her.

They came from the opposite end of the warehouse behind a stack of crates. She scooted farther down the stairs and dove to the side, rolling behind a stack of crates she hoped weren't loaded with explosives.

A second later and another barrage of shots came, ripping her barrier apart. That meant the guard had a higher position, probably on top of the crates, and was firing at a downward angle. She shifted along the edge of her box.

She rolled around the side, took aim, and released a dart at where she thought the man would be hiding.

A thud told her she had found her mark.

And then everything went silent.

7

Lyle crouched against the wall, in plain sight and not caring. He was terrified, especially now that guns were being discharged, and he didn't know what to do.

He held a pistol in his shaking hand, but the safety was still on. For the life of him, he couldn't figure out how to get it off.

This was a gunfight.

A real gunfight.

If anyone so much as glanced his way, they would see a terrified man cowering and trying not to cry, and they would laugh.

Or he hoped they would laugh. The alternative was much worse.

"Lyle," he heard, but couldn't move.

Kate had to repeat his name three times for him to face her. She was ducked behind a box and waving at him. She was whispering loudly to get his attention.

"Stop whispering."

"Then start paying attention."

"If you use a hushed voice instead of a whisper the sound won't travel as far."

"What the hell good does knowing that do me right now?"

He shrugged and crawled toward her.

"I think most of them are down," she said. "Heavy tranquilizer darts, so they will be out for a few hours. But if you see any of them lying on the ground, shoot them again just in case."

"Like, to kill them?"

"No, you have a dart gun."

"This is a dart gun?" he asked, holding it up. "It looks so real."

"It *is* real."

"I meant...you *know* what I meant," he said, chagrined.

She laughed. "Of course, I did. Now shut up and follow me."

He stumbled drunkenly behind her she moved through the warehouse. He was sweating.

"Are you okay?" she asked.

He giggled. "No. Not even a little bit. I think I'm going to die from shock."

"You have to get shot first."

"Oh? Is that how it works?"

"There are two more guards at least, and by now they know we are here."

"Okay."

"I'm going to cover you from the railing, and I need you to move slowly toward the front doors until you find Jack's family."

"Okay," he said.

She reached over and flicked a switch on his gun. "Safety off. If you see anyone, shoot them."

"Okay," he muttered again.

A long moment passed as he stared at the wall and she stared at him.

Finally, he met her gaze and grimaced. "You mean now?"

"Of course, I mean now. When else?"

"I don't know. I wasn't really paying attention."

She groaned and pointed toward the front entrance of the warehouse. "Sneak that way and don't get shot."

He forced himself to breathe deeply to make the stars go away. He walked in a crouch toward the front of the warehouse, weaving around boxes and trying not to breathe too loudly.

His movements were jerky and awkward. His legs felt like rubber. He didn't want to be here. He wanted to be anywhere but here, and the only thing that kept him moving was the thought that Kate was protecting him.

She wouldn't allow him to do anything *really* dangerous, right?

8

Kate didn't like using Lyle as bait, but it seemed like the best idea at the time.

She tightened her grip on the rifle and scanned around. She'd spotted two other people near the front of the warehouse, but they hadn't moved when fighting began. If she had to guess, that was Jack's family.

Hopefully, they weren't dead.

She watched the doors and windows as Lyle moved at

snail's pace along the ground. Nothing happened for a full minute, and she was on edge. Her nerves would betray her if she wasn't careful.

She waited, rifle at the ready.

After what felt an eternity, she saw movement near the far left wall of the building. One of the access doors slid open and a form stepped into the warehouse.

She lined up a shot, waited for movement, and pulled the trigger. The form slumped to the ground.

9

Each time he got to a corner, he did the James Bond corner look before stepping around it. He wished he had a mirror to do the mirror trick where you hold it up to look down the hallway.

Hell, he wished he wasn't here at all.

His hands wouldn't stop shaking and his breath was coming in short ragged bursts. When he finally made it to the front of the warehouse he was lightheaded and dizzy.

Two people were in the center of the clearing tied to chairs, and a car seat sat near them with a baby sleeping inside.

Lyle scanned the area and then walked over to the people.

"Are you Jack?" he asked.

Jack's eyes went wide. "Watch—"

Lyle spun. He saw a man come around the corner with a machine gun.

Leveled right at him.

Lyle started to raise his pistol but way too slowly. He knew he was dead. He closed his eyes and grimaced.

Except he didn't die. He raised his pistol and fired, eyes still closed. Then he fired again, and again.

He fired at least six times. When he opened them, the man slumped against the boxes, four darts in his chest.

Lyle stood there, panting and gasping for air, trying not to try. A moment passed, and then he stepped forward to look at the man who had almost killed him. There were darts all over him and he looked like he was barely breathing.

"Oops," he said.

"Oops is right," Kate said, stepping around the corner.

Lyle raised his gun to fire, but his sweaty palms betrayed him and it slipped out of his grasp. He tried to catch it, swatted it again, and then he heard a *pssh* sound as his gun fired.

Time froze as he stood there. When he looked up, Kate had a look on her face of mixed shock and amusement. She was staring at his chest.

When he looked down, he saw a dart sticking out of his shirt, wavering there.

He looked back at Kate, feeling wobbly. She smiled at him.

"Oops," she agreed.

And then the world went dark.

Chapter 13
Arizona

1

Kate sat on the curbside, elbow on her knee and chin resting on her hand. Her clothes had the faint aroma of dried sweat but she wasn't sure how long it would be before she managed a shower.

She noticed Lyle stepping out of the hotel. He walked across the street toward her, yawning.

"Hey, sleepyhead," she said.

"Very funny."

"I haven't seen anyone tranq themselves before," she added. "But I guess that's one way to get a good night's rest."

"Har, har," he said. "You are just *so* funny.

"You'll be tired for a while, but it'll wear off after you have some coffee."

"Good to know."

"How are Jack and Marian doing?"

"Marian stopped crying," Lyle replied.

Kate nodded. "That's good."

"Once Jack calmed down, he said he knew what the target was going to be," Lyle said.

Kate perked up. "Seriously?"

"A city in Texas. Fairly low population."

"Does he know where they are?"

"No," Lyle said. "They made him wear a bag before taking him to the warehouse. He was in an abandoned police station, but they were packing up like they were about to leave."

"Damn," she replied. "So we know the target, we just don't know how to stop them."

Lyle hesitated. "I might have an idea on how we can do that."

"What?"

"Let me look into it some more, and I'll get back to you."

2

The black truck pulled to a stop behind the police station. Francis was outside waiting for them. Victor climbed out into the alley.

"Go inside," he said to William. "And get Helen and Beck. We're leaving."

"Sure," William said, disappearing into the station.

Victor turned to Francis after he was gone. "What is it?"

In response, Francis handed him a phone. "It's cued up."

Victor hit play on it. "...little town called Cottonwood Heights," Helen's voice said, tinny on the speakers.

Victor stopped the recording, feeling his body shaking with anger.

"When was this?"

"Not long after you went to get Jack's family," Francis said. "We were doing a perimeter sweep."

"She told Beck?"

"She told Jack as well," Francis said.

Victor growled and dialed into the phone. "I'm going to have them kill Jack and bury him in the desert."

"He's military."

"He's a liability."

Francis didn't argue. Victor held the phone up, but it kept ringing. After the tenth ring, he yelled and threw the phone into the wall.

"That stupid bitch!"

"They didn't answer?" Francis asked calmly.

"No," Victor replied. "They have been compromised."

"Who do you think it is?"

"I don't know," Victor said. "JanCorp has a lot of enemies. We have a lot of enemies. The list is long."

"Do you want me to check it you?"

Victor shook his head. "No. The warehouse is gone. Jack is gone. We need to move forward and finish this. We will assume whoever is working against us knows the target, so we'll meet them there and deal with them."

"Helen is on the Air Force network now," Francis said. "Beck helped her breach inside and we can take control of the drones."

"Did you show Helen the recording?"

"No," Francis said. "Do you want me to kill her?"

Victor took a deep breath. "Yes. But first, let's get paid."

3

Kate brushed the hair out of her eyes, having to pee but knowing it wouldn't be a possibility just yet. Marian sequestered herself inside the shower as soon as they entered the hotel, and the only positive development in the situation was that she'd finally allowed Jack to come inside with her.

Kate was working on her laptop but gave up hunting for leads and was spending time reading up on any information about Cottonwood Heights. That was the target of the drone attack, but it was a little backwater town.

It was also a long way from any military installations that could deal with the threat.

"Why there?"

"What?" Lyle asked, sitting on the other bed, lost in thought.

"Cottonwood Heights It sounds familiar, but I can't place it. I know I've heard the name before."

"Maybe they don't want many casualties," Lyle replied. "It doesn't have a huge population."

She shook her head. "They want to make a big splash," she argued. "Casualties are their number one priority. The thing I can't figure out is, who is paying for this?"

"Maybe they want to start a war," Lyle offered.

"What do you mean?"

"You said JanCorp spent a lot of time working in the Middle East. They weren't picky about which side they worked for, right?"

Kate felt her eyes go wide. "Oh no."

"What is it?"

Kate started typing. "The US recruited a lot of locals in the Middle East to help, turning them against their country and government. A lot of them were brought to the US in exchange for what they did."

"Okay," Lyle said.

"The highest priority ones are usually given false identities and hidden, similar to witness protection because the people they betrayed back home wanted them dead."

"We gave them asylum."

"A lot we abandoned back home because there wasn't enough money to bring them, but many important or noteworthy ones were brought into the states."

"You think one of these might be the target?"

"I think it could be several," she said. "Sometimes groups were moved over together to make it easier to keep track of them and help blend in. They form communities and live in close proximity to their families. It's a way to get a clean start."

"Cottonwood Heights," Lyle said. "You think it's sheltering Middle Easterners who turned their backs on their nations."

Kate nodded. "I know it is. JanCorp helped put them there."

4

"Then why would they want to kill them?" Lyle asked.

"Because they're being paid. These people are viewed as traitors by some back home, and there is good money in finding and killing them. Victor is working for either a government or a rebel group who wants these people killed, and they want it done in as public a fashion as possible."

"A public execution."

She nodded. "They want possible defectors in the future to see the trust cost of betraying their countries."

"But these are families, right?" he asked. "Not just the people who helped the US."

"That's part of the plan," she said. "Just killing the people isn't enough."

Lyle was silent for a long moment. "That's horrible."

"But it gives us an idea of what their plan is," Kate added. "Now we just have to figure out how to stop them."

Chapter 14
Cottonwood Heights

1

"It's going to make it a lot harder to do the hack."

"We had to get moving," Victor said, loading gear into the back of the brown VW Francis had stolen. It would blend in well as they headed southeast to their destination. "Staying in one place too long is dangerous."

Helen didn't want to go with them. She didn't want to be anywhere near Victor, and the more time she spent with him and his team, the more worried she became that he was on to her. Did he know why she requested to join his team?

She was starting to think that the tip she received all those weeks ago was true: Victor had killed her sister.

"I should stay here to finish the hack," Helen argued. "I'm no use to you on the road."

"We are all staying together until this is through," Victor replied, finality in his voice. "And if I have to ask you to pack your gear one more time, I'll put a bullet in your head and find another hacker to finish this."

Helen's lip quivered. She knew Victor didn't like to be messed with, but she didn't know much else. He was dangerous, and she doubted it was an idle threat. *Does he know what I told Jack and Beck?*

Not that it would matter. Beck was still in the office, tied to a chair, and Jack had been shuffled off to another location under guard. Her little spur of the moment rebellion wouldn't accomplish anything.

At least, they didn't know, and as long as Beck kept his mouth shut it should be fine.

"Give me five minutes," she said.

"You have two," Victor replied, walking away.

It wouldn't be easy to get all of her gear packed, and with them traveling it would be more difficult to maintain satellite connections, but she would manage.

That wasn't what concerned her, anyway. She was more worried about the fact that they were traveling to the target area where they would launch the missiles. Even if they stayed out of the blast radius, it was a lot closer to ground zero than she would like.

But she didn't have much choice.

"Looks like I'm going to Cottonwood."

2

Lyle sat in the passenger seat with Kate's laptop open, reading as much information as he could about the layout of Cottonwood and surrounding areas.

"What are you looking at?" she asked.

"The town layout," Lyle said. "I'm trying to figure out where their target will be?"

"We don't want to be anywhere near the target," Kate agreed.

"What kind of building was it?" Lyle asked. "Where JanCorp put the people they brought from the Middle East."

"I'm not sure," Kate said. "But usually apartments."

"There are three apartment complexes," Lyle said. "And they are each a few miles from each other."

"Does it show contractors who built them?"

"Yeah," Lyle said.

"Are any Ashton constructing?"

Lyle scanned it. "One is."

"Then that is the target," she said.

Lyle kept looking at the surrounding area, finally pinpointing a building nearby that would be tall enough for his purposes. "This one," he said. "I'll give you the address."

"How can you read like that?"

"Hmm?" Lyle asked.

Kate was driving. Jack was in the backseat, half asleep and staring out the window. He'd all but demanded they let him come. His wife objected, but she could tell he wasn't going to listen. He felt like he'd helped cause this, so it was his duty to help fix it.

"Reading in a car makes me sick," Kate explained.

"It used to make me throw up too," Lyle said with a shrug. "But then I grew out of it."

"Do you get seasick?"

"Worse than you can imagine," Lyle said. "And airsick sometimes. How far out are we?"

"Another fifty miles."

"We need to stop at a hardware store."

"Why?"

"Supplies," he said.

"What kind of supplies?"

He glanced over at her. "The kind I need to build an EMP."

"A what?"

"Electromagnetic pulse," Lyle explained.

"I know what it is," she said. "How is it going to help us?"

"I'm going to use it to bring down the drones."

"Seriously?"

"It isn't that hard when you get down to it. Basically, I just need to push a lot of electricity through copper wires, more than they can handle and bridge it so most of it ends up in the atmosphere."

"Ah."

"The real problem is going to be the power supply."

"What do you mean?"

"Well," Lyle said. "I need to figure out how to hijack the local power grid without electrocuting myself."

3

"I'm in the network," Helen said. She was riding the backseat of the car next to Beck, who was tied up with duct tape, and

Francis. The lithe mercenary was quiet, barely speaking a word the entire trip. Beck was morose and exhausted, giving her pleading looks. She ignored him.

They were still eighty or ninety miles out from their destination. William was driving and Victor was riding shotgun. He hadn't calmed down and seemed on the verge of exploding at any moment. Helen was doing her best not to piss him off.

"You're on their network?" Victor asked.

"I'm in both networks now. Markwell and the Air Force. Once I take the drone from the Air Force, I can swap it to Markwell and lock them out."

"Are any drones in the air nearby Cottonwood Heights?"

"Five," she said. "Border patrol drones flying as a squad, all carrying predator missiles. Should I hijack one?"

"No," he decided. "Take all five."

Chapter 15
Cottonwood Heights

1

It took Helen another five or so minutes to hijack control of the drones. The car jostled down the road and Beck hung his head in consternation, miserable in the seat beside her. Victor watched from the front seat, eyes on her at all moments.

"I've got them," Helen said. "Putting them into formation to fly to Cottonwood Heights."

"How long?"

"A little over an hour," she said. "Right now no one knows what happened, and they might just think it's a glitch."

"We'll be there about the same time," William said.

Victor looked at Helen in the rearview mirror.

"Drive faster," he ordered.

It was awkward in the car. William had turned the radio on when they first started driving, but Victor had switched it off without a word. Now they exchanged glances and occasionally someone coughed.

All of the drone safety measures would be locked out by the Markwell system. Once the first attempts by the Air Force failed to reinstitute control over their drones, they would shut off the entire network and lock everyone out in a full restart. It wouldn't do any good, however, and Helen would still be able to control the drones.

They wouldn't even understand how bad it really was until it was too late.

She wanted to ask if it was really necessary to hijack all five drones. Even with a military installation, one drone should have enough firepower to do as much damage as they needed to be done.

"Is the upload stream ready?" Victor asked.

"We can stream video from the drones to our employer as soon as we are ready," Helen replied. "They'll be able to watch the attack in real time."

"Good," Victor replied. "Open it to the public as well."

"What?" Helen asked, shocked. "What do you mean?"

"Open the stream to everyone," Victor said. "Create an open URL. Let's broadcast it to as many people as want to watch."

Helen hesitated. It wouldn't be hard to do: she would open a feed through Tor networks and connect it to the drones. By the time anyone had found out where the feed was coming from they would be long gone.

It was just...it felt wrong. It was one thing to watch violence on the television when it was make believe. It was another thing entirely to give everyone access to real violence.

"I'll see what I can do," she said. "It'll take a few minutes."

"It had better be up before we arrive in Cottonwood," Victor said. "I want the world to witness this."

Helen bit back her response. She didn't like the idea of killing anyone, but making a show of it...

Still, the question was: was she more afraid of doing something horrible, or Victor?

She would need to get out of this as soon as she could.

2

Lyle jumped out of the car as soon as it rolled to a stop in front of the abandoned office building. It had been closed to renovation several years ago when the contractor ran out of funding and left in disrepair ever since. The city would eventually tear it down, but for now, it was a forgotten landmark just outside of town.

He opened the trunk and started grabbing wires.

"Help me carry this all up to the roof," Lyle said, picking up a power regulator. "It's heavy."

Kate picked up one of the long wires, groaning under the weight. "No kidding."

Jack picked up another roll of copper wire and followed. "What do we need all of this for?"

"I'm going to form it into coils," Lyle said, "and then hook it into the grid. I'll use the regulator to up the amps, and when we turn it on it should release a pretty good blast."

"It'll take out the drones?"

Lyle nodded. "It should, in theory."

"In theory?"

"If these drones are insulated then it won't do a lot of good. But that isn't common practice because it's expensive as hell and makes them weigh almost twice as much, so this should work just fine."

They trekked up the stairs to the roof. The staircase doubled back on each flight in the stairwell and was rough in some places where construction hadn't been completed. All three were panting by the time they made it up. Lyle started setting up, and Kate and Jack headed back down to get the remainder of the supplies.

"Do you think this is going to work?" Jack asked Kate on the way down.

"Nope," Kate said. "But it isn't the plan anyway."

"What's the plan?"

"Find the people responsible for this and get them to shut it down before anyone gets killed."

"You think they will be here?"

"I think at least one of them will be on site," Kate said. "They'll want to have boots on the ground, especially now that we got you out."

"You think they know I'm gone?"

"I'm sure they knew almost as soon as it happened. They'll be looking for us."

Jack slung a large metal device over his shoulder and grunted. "Then why are we doing *this*?"

Kate picked up the last roll of wires and a bag of tools and followed Jack back toward the stairs. "Because it's always worth having a backup plan, even if it's an insane one."

3

William parked the VW about half a mile outside Cottonwood Heights. He found a dirt road with a good vantage of the city and their target. Dust hung in the air behind them from their tires, floating away gently in the breeze.

"This is a good spot," Victor said.

"Want us to set a perimeter?"

He shook his head. He moved William and Francis away from the car while Helen pulled out her gear. "I want you both to head into town and find out who's after us."

"Want them alive?" William asked.

"I want them dead," Victor said. "I want them to suffer, but I want them dead."

Francis eyed him. "You going to be all right here alone?"

"I'll be fine," Victor said.

"All right," Francis said. They grabbed their pistols and started walking toward town, leaving Victor with Helen and Beck.

Helen set her computer on the hood of the car, swapping controls to keep all of the drones heading in the same direction. Beck was out of the backseat, but his hands were still tied. He leaned against the car and watched, morose and beaten.

Victor watched her, eyes cold and dead. "Keep them in formation," he said.

"It's harder than it looks," Helen said, adjusting the screens and swapping between the various controls. "I have to make constant tiny changes to each of them to make sure they don't crash into each other."

"Is the camera streaming?"

"Yes."

"Use the farthest one back. I want it to show the others

firing their missiles."

"Okay," she said. Victor felt himself smiling slightly, watching her suffer. She hated this, but she didn't have the strength to object. He would enjoy killing her but not nearly as much as her firebrand sister. "How far out are they?"

"Ten minutes," Helen said. "Ten minutes until you can fire the missiles."

4

By the time Jack and Kate made it back to the roof, Lyle had put together a pretty significant contraption. It looked like an art sculpture made out of copper wires, each strand wrapped around the others as it reached for the sky.

"Looks like a child made that," Kate said. Lyle gave her a dirty look.

"I'd like to see you do better in such a short time span."

"I don't even know what you're doing," she said.

"I agree. What the *hell* is that?" Jack asked.

"It's an EMP," Lyle said.

"Why is it so big?"

"Because we need to run a huge current through it," Lyle replied. He mentioned it like it should be obvious.

Jack turned to Kate, shaking his head. "I'm going to head down and try to warn the people in the target area. If we can get people out of harm's way, then even if they do fire missiles it won't do much harm."

"Okay," Kate said. "But if the drones get too close then get the hell out of there."

"All right," Jack said. He headed back to the stairs and disappeared.

Kate turned back to Lyle. "You almost done?"

"Almost," Lyle said. He saw the bag of tools Kate had brought and grabbed one out. He hurried to his sculpture and started snipping the copper wire in various places.

"What are you doing?"

"Creating air gaps," Lyle explained. "We want the current to jump so that a most of it ends up in the air. That's what creates the pulse...hypothetically."

"Hypothetically?"

"This was all Tesla stuff, and I've never built something like this before. I'm not great with electrical currents so I can only hope it works. The regulator should get us a huge jolt, and the pulse will go pretty far. If we time it right, it should fry the electronics on the drones."

Kate sighed. "So it *might* work?"

"It might," Lyle said. "Or...it might just explode."

5

"Head into town and find out who made those footprints," Francis said to William as they stood near the tall building outside of town. They had found a car parked outside of it, and Francis would bet anything that whoever was working against them had been driving it.

He didn't know why they were here, at this building, unless maybe they had the wrong target. He didn't particularly care, either.

They had found a pair of footsteps as well in the sandy gravel outside the building, heading toward town.

"Who am I looking for?"

"Just keep your eyes peeled," Francis said. "If you see anything odd, call me."

"All right," William said.

He started lumbering toward the city, following the footsteps in almost comical incompetence. Francis watched him go with distaste and let out a deep sigh.

William was useless on a job like this. He didn't want the person in the building to know he was here, so sending William away was the only real option he had. He doubted William would see anything in the city, but at least, it kept him busy.

He slid his pistol free, clicked the safety off, and crept into the building. There was a stairwell just inside and he headed up. He moved slowly, stepping quietly and listening. By the fourth landing, he could hear voices as someone walked into the stairwell above him, a few flights higher up.

"...it still dangerous, even if it works?" a woman asked.

"I don't think so," a man replied. "Tesla never said anything about it. I mean, it might cause cancer, but what doesn't?"

"True."

"Besides, that's why I got the remote. It has half a mile range, so we don't have to be anywhere close when we click it."

Francis moved farther into the building, hiding around a corner on the fourth-floor landing. He held his pistol and waited.

6

Kate walked down the stairs beside Lyle. He held the remote in his hand, little more than a switch. She held hope that they wouldn't have to use it and figured if Lyle actually had to throw that switch his great device would just flash with sparks and sputter out.

But, at least, he was trying. She was impressed with how composed he was through all of this. He'd been through a lot in the last day, and somehow he was holding himself together.

"I'm sorry," she said.

"For what?" he asked.

"If I'd left you in the hotel with the FBI, you probably could have convinced them you were innocent with the evidence you found. I basically ruined any chance you had of clearing your name."

He let out a sigh and stopped walking.

"Maybe," he said. "But it still would have been a longshot. But, the thing is, I don't hold you responsible for anything. None of it was your fault, and if anything you've given me a chance to do something good."

"What do you mean?" she asked.

"I'm a coward."

"No you aren't," she replied. "I've met cowards, and you aren't one of them."

"But I am," he said. "I spent my life writing code that helps people kill other people from a distance. They are planning to kill thousands of people with barely any effort, and that is partly my fault."

"But you're here."

"Exactly," he replied. "I'm here because of *you*. I was too scared to tell anyone about the Markwell back door because I was coward, and now my best friend is dead. You've saved my life and given me the chance to redeem myself, if only a little bit. Thank you."

She hesitated. "You're welcome."

"I just wanted to say that—"

"It's my sister," Kate said suddenly. Lyle trailed off. "I got her into this life, got her a job at JanCorp. She's just following in my footsteps, and now she's in danger."

They started walking down the stairs again, heading from the fifth landing.

"Can't you just get her out?"

"She's working with the people who tried to kill me," Kate said.

A figure suddenly stepped out of the shadows inside the fourth-floor landing, grabbing Lyle's wrist and taking the remote. He dropped it on the floor and stepped on it, smashing the components.

Then he looked up at Kate and laughed. "We obviously didn't try hard enough."

7

Kate reached for her gun, but the man put his own to Lyle's head.

"Don't even think about it."

"Francis," Kate breathed, holding her hands to the side. "Let him go, he has nothing to do with this."

"You know, I thought it was cute when your sister asked to work with us. Sort of poetic, working with her to hunt down the people who killed you, and she would never know that those were the same people helping her."

"But she didn't trust you," Kate replied.

"Not once," Francis said. "Too much like her sister."

"I trusted you for years," Kate said. "Then you stabbed me in the back."

"That's the thing about it," Francis explained. "It always comes down to the money."

Kate felt like she'd been punched in the stomach. "There was a price on my head?"

"A pretty big one," Francis said. "A bonus we made off of our last job with you."

"Who was it?" Kate asked.

Francis shrugged. "I never found out. They only worked with Victor."

"Then you already collected," Kate said.

"Yeah," he said. "Speaking of which."

A second later, he placed his pistol against Lyle's stomach and pulled the trigger. Then he shoved Lyle forward into Kate. He screamed in pain and flailed, making it difficult for her to draw her own gun. He got it loose and raised up, tracking Francis, but he was already halfway down the stairs, heading for the exit.

Kate quick stepped after him, raising her pistol and firing. Francis ducked around the next landing and the bullets thudded around him.

"Stay here," she said to Lyle. "I'll be right back."

Then she headed down the stairs, chasing Francis.

Chapter 16
Cottonwood Heights

1

Kate jumped the railing on the second floor, landing a short distance behind him. Francis, firing off two quick shots and forcing Kate to scramble back. She slapped his gun to the side and ducked, hitting him with a tackle.

They both rolled down the stairs in a heap, grunting from the rough stairs. She busted her hand pretty good but managed to keep a grip on her pistol.

He kneed her in the stomach, and she kicked his ankle as they rolled apart. He fired again then dropped over the railing to the bottom floor below. He fired up at her but then his gun clicked empty.

Kate dove after him, landing hard on the cement floor, and raised her gun. Francis sprinted for the exit and she fired again, hitting him in the hip. He staggered into the wall and disappeared around the corner.

She chased him. As soon as she stepped outside he ambushed her, swinging a wooden beam at her head. She ducked and stepped back, dodging another clumsy attack.

He pursued her, staggering forward and swinging the beam, and she kept backpedaling, knowing he wouldn't be able to go for long.

He hit the doorway behind her, dropped the beam, and punched her in the shoulder. She rolled with the punch, stepped in, and kicked his knee. He went down and she punched out for his hip, hoping to hit him where the bullet lodged.

He was quicker than she expected, though, and instead she felt him hit her in the neck. She staggered to the ground, rolling away from him and then swept his legs. He went down hard with a groan and she rolled away from him.

She rolled to her feet, grabbed the beam, and brought it down hard against his knee, shattering it. He screamed in pain, clutching the broken tendons.

"Don't move," she said, picking up her gun and leveling it at him.

"What do you want?" he asked, choking and sobbing from the pain.

"Where is Victor?" she asked.

"You think I would tell you?"

"No, I didn't really think you would," she said. "Just had to ask."

She pulled the trigger, putting a bullet right between his eyes.

2

Jack slipped into the apartment building on the first floor and looked around. It was well maintained and bustling with activity. Several sleepy looking people sat in the foyer and some kids were in the corner playing a game.

He wandered down the hallway. A lot of people gave him curious glances, knowing he was an outsider in multiple cases.

Once he turned the corner into a fairly empty hallway, he glanced around until he saw a fire alarm. He walked over to it casually, lifted the flap and pulled it down, then kept walking down the hall. The alarm started blaring, ringing through the hallway.

It was also attached to the sprinklers and suddenly they released, raining water down on the hallway. He was soaked in seconds.

He heard people shouting behind him and kept walking, heading for the exit. A door opened up beside him and an old man peeked out. The man asked him something in a language he didn't understand, then in English said, "What's going on?"

Jack opened his mouth to speak just as the gunshot went

off.

He didn't know he'd been hit right away. The bullet clipped his shoulder, but he heard the roar from the hand cannon behind him in the hallway. He turned and saw the huge man who had helped kidnap him standing there. Kate had told him the brute's name was William.

William had just rounded the corner behind him. He was holding a massive gun and looked pissed off.

Jack didn't think, just reacted. He dove to the side, pushing past the old man into the apartment just as the gun roared again. It took out a sizeable chunk of the wall but didn't hit him.

Then he was inside the room. He dodged around a coffee table into the kitchen. The old man was yelling at him and the alarm continued to blare.

He heard William crash into the room a second later, shouting curses. Another gunshot, well behind Jack, and he ducked into a side room. He bumped into a cabinet, knocking glass sculptures all over the floor and then pushed the entire thing over to partially block the doorway.

Then he ran to the window and slid it open. He felt his heart thumping in his chest and it seemed like he needed to vomit, but he forced himself to keep moving.

He got the window open and slipped outside just as William came into sight. He glanced back and saw the huge man shouting and raising his pistol.

But, more disconcerting, Jack saw blood smeared all over the windowsill behind him.

His blood.

He ducked around the corner just as William shot again, sending up flashes of debris into his face as the bullet smashed through the wall.

People were shouting and flooding outside, some pointed in his direction. A woman screamed.

Dripping water and blood and shoulder throbbing, Jack stumbled down the road and away from William.

3

Kate heard the gunshots and knew Jack was in trouble. She desperately wanted to go check on Lyle, who she feared might be dying on the stairs above her, but she knew if she left Jack alone he would be dead in only moments. She hurried back into the building to the foot of the stairs.

"Stay awake, Lyle," she shouted, cupping her hands around her mouth. "Whatever you do, stay conscious."

Then she ran back out into the sun. She jumped into the car and sped down the road, heading for where she heard the gunshots.

4

Jack was exhausted, feeling his adrenaline wearing out. His arm hurt and his shirt was matted against his body. William wouldn't stop coming. Just shouting behind him. They had been running for little longer than a minute through the streets and alleys, but the high intensity was debilitating.

William behind him wasn't doing so hot either. He'd run out of bullets, wasting all of his shots and then thrown the gun away. Now he was focused entirely on catching Jack.

"Come back here, you little worm!" William shouted, chasing him back out to the main thoroughfare. Jack staggered along, dodging pedestrians and holding his arm.

Sirens blared some distance away, but Jack knew it would be a while before they arrived. Too long to help him.

He turned down another alley. As soon as he had stepped a few feet in he knew he'd made a mistake. It dead ended about a quarter of a mile at a brick wall. He knew it was too late to turn back, though, because William was only a few steps behind him.

He knocked over a stack of boxes leaning against a trash can, hoping to block the way. But they were empty boxes, too light to cause real obstruction. William plowed right through them, grunting.

Jack saw a fire escape ladder, but it was out of reach. There was a trashcan nearby he could use to jump up to the ladder. He slid it into space, climbed awkwardly on top and then jumped up to grab the ladder with his good arm.

It held for a second before releasing the clasp and sliding down. Jack held on for a second, then it jolted about halfway down and he fell loose.

He hit the ground with a loud expulsion of air, groaning and rolled to his feet. William stopped a few feet short and burst out laughing.

"Didn't think that through, did you?"

Jack rolled awkwardly to his feet, picking up the lid of the trashcan. He held it in front of him like a shield, keeping it between him and William.

"Stay back," he muttered, panting.

William laughed again. "What are you going to do with that?"

"I saw Captain America," Jack said. "I know how to use this."

"I'm going to shove that shield so far up—"

The sound of a car roaring around the corner filled the alley. William turned just in time to see a little brown vehicle come flying forward. It slammed into him with a resounding thud, sending him rolling down the alley in a heap.

Jack stood near the wall, panting, as William came to a stop in front of him. He was groaning and shifting but barely able to move. The burly man looked half delirious as he tried to stand.

Jack hit him in the head with his trash can shield, knocking him back down. Blood spurted from his nose, and Jack was fairly certain he'd broken it.

Kate climbed out of the car and walked over to William, carrying a pistol. The sirens were getting closer but still too far away.

"You look like hell," she mentioned to Jack as she passed.

"You don't exactly look perfect yourself," he said. She had a bloody lip and look scuffed up like she'd been in a fight.

She shrugged. "I guess it's just one of those days."

William was rolling, clutching his broken nose. She stepped on his leg as he tried to crawl away and pressed the end of the pistol against his head. He roared in pain but fell silent when he felt the gun.

"Francis is already dead," Kate said. "So you have two seconds to tell me where Victor is, Bill."

Chapter 17
Cottonwood Heights

1

"There's a problem," Helen said.

"With the drones?" Victor asked.

"With the target," Helen replied. "You said it was a military installation."

"And?"

"There are no bases around here," she said, "and the coordinate you gave me are for an apartment complex."

Victor didn't reply.

Helen tapped at the computer, her eyes going wide. "You knew."

He leveled his gaze at her. "Get back to work."

"No," she said. "I refuse to be a part of this."

"Don't you dare disobey me," Victor said.

"Screw you," Helen said.

Victor drew his gun in one smooth motion, turned, and fired at Beck. The bullet hit the drone pilot in the leg, and he collapsed to the ground screaming.

Victor shifted it again and this time, he aimed it at Beck's head. "Want me to fire again?"

Helen felt her lip quiver. "You're crazy."

"Maybe."

"You'll kill me if I don't help you?"

"No, first I'll kill Beck. But I'm not going to kill you, Helen. There are worse things."

"Like what."

"I've seen the picture you look at. Your dead sister. You loved her and looked up to her. You wanted to be like her. But you aren't. You know why? Your sister was a heartless bitch who knew how to do her job. She didn't cry and moan about how bad things were. She got things done."

"Leave Kate out of this," Helen said softly.

"I can't," Victor said, "because I'm the one who killed her."

He savored the look of confused rage on Helen's face as she processed the information.

"Why?" she asked.

"Because she was in my way," Victor said. "And when things are in my way, I take care of them. Now, I'm going to ask you a very important question, and I would think long and hard about your answer: are you in my way?"

Beck writhed on the ground, clutching his leg and groaning.

Helen stared at Victor, body tense like she was about to strike. "You'll just kill me if I'm in your way?" she asked.

Victor laughed. "Oh no, I won't kill you. I'll cripple you and then I will punish you. I already killed your sister, which means you don't have a lot of family left. What about your mom? If you don't help me, I'll go find her next, and kill her. Cousins, uncles, aunts, I'll kill them too. I'll kill everyone you love and care about until you are alone in this world.

"Starting with him," Victor finished, cocking the hammer back on his pistol and nodding at Beck. "Now. Get. To. Work."

Helen stared at him a second longer before letting out a shuddering breath. On the verge of tears and hands shaking, she started typing the firing sequence commands into her laptop.

Victor released the hammer on his pistol.

"That's what I thought."

2

Lyle crawled up the stairs, leaving a trail of blood behind him. He used his left hand to pull himself up and the right to hold his stomach. It was difficult to breathe and his vision was starting to fade any out. The pain was nauseating, and he felt like he was going to pass out at any second, but he pressed on.

"Stay conscious, she says," he mumbled. He tried to laugh but ended up coughing instead. "How could I fall asleep with all this excitement?"

He kept crawling.

He had tried counting the steps as he passed them, but he couldn't string the numbers together. He couldn't even remember what floor he was on now. His reality had become a lot simpler as he went: left arm up on the next stair, pull his body, left arm up on the next stair, pull his body, repeat.

He kept crawling.

Lyle wasn't even sure what he was doing. The device had been broken and he couldn't remotely trigger his device. He wasn't even sure he could make it to the roof in time to even see the drones flying overhead.

But he kept thinking about all of the people in the apartment complex. The children who would be killed if the missiles were fired. If there was even the slightest chance he would stop it from happening, then wasn't it worth trying?

He kept crawling.

Suddenly there was a door in front of him, hanging open. He was on the roof. The sun was overwhelmingly bright and he let out a gasp as his eyes adjusted. Breathing was getting more difficult with each passing second.

The device he'd built still had a manual switch. He could trigger the EMP as long as he was close enough to flip that switch.

"Maybe it'll just blow up," Lyle said. "At least, it'll stop hurting."

Left arm, pull, left arm, pull. He thought it would be easier on the roof, now that he was on level ground. But it was actually more difficult.

He had lost a lot of blood. He didn't know how much, but he felt lightheaded and the pain was starting to diminish. That was what worried him the most. If it hurt less, then that probably meant he was losing the ability to process the pain. He wouldn't be able to hold on much longer.

He could hear the drones now in the distance. They were closing in.

So he crawled. He could see his contraption, mere feet away near the edge of the building, but it felt like he was crossing a barren wasteland to reach it.

Chapter 18
Cottonwood Heights

1

Victor saw the car approaching in the distance, kicking up dust as it went. He knew without even having a clear view that it wasn't Francis or William driving it. It was coming too fast.

Which meant it was someone coming to stop him.

"Is it ready?" he asked.

"The commands are set and the target is locked," Helen said, her voice morose. Beck was still writhing on the ground in agony, but Victor had little trouble ignoring him. "They will fire as soon as they are in range."

"And it requires no further input to fire and transmit?"

"None," Helen said. "It's done."

Victor glanced back at the approaching car, wondering what had happened to Francis and William. Were they dead? It would be unfortunate, but that was the cost of this life.

The car was only a few hundred meters away. Victor shifted and fired his pistol into the laptop. He fired several shots, destroying it, and then faced back to the car.

"Now it's done," he said.

The car came in fast. Victor lined up where the driver would be and fired out several shots. The window splintered and cracked where he hit, but he couldn't tell if he'd made contact with his shots. The car didn't stop, however, but only sped up. It barreled down on his position.

About twenty feet away it swerved on the dirt road, sliding at an angle and kicking up a huge wave of dust. It floated in, covering him completely. Victor squinted through the cloud, looking for the car. He heard Helen cough next to him but kept focused on the car. He heard the driver door open and fired blindly at that.

Footsteps approached, crunching the dirt. He aimed and fired blindly again. Suddenly a shape appeared out of the dust cloud. He was instantly on the defensive, blocking a punch to his face and knee to his groin. He stumbled back, trying to put distance between him and his attacker.

The gun was knocked out of his hand and he staggered back. A hit landed solidly on his leg, and he collapsed to one knee. He launched a clumsy counterattack and was easily deflected. He fought back up and kept moving back, trying to get out of the cloud.

The dust hung in the air, making it difficult to see. He stayed on the defensive, backpedaling and avoiding strikes. It was hard to make out the features of his attacker other than it was a slight woman. She moved fast and with grace.

He dodged another kick, felt his legs get swept out from under him, and suddenly he was on his back with the air knocked out of his lungs.

That was followed a second later by a kick to his face, disorienting him. He tried to stagger back to his feet and felt a kick in his ribs, throwing him back down.

The dust floated away, and he was able to see again. He tried to crawl away. Another kick to the ribs sent him down, and he rolled over.

His eyes went wide.

"You!" he said, coughing. "I killed you!"

Kate stood overtop him, holding a gun and with a pissed off expression on her face.

"Next time check for a body."

She shot him in the stomach. He felt searing pain and let out a scream from the pain.

"Who put the hit out on me?" she asked.

Victor tried to crawl away, but she walked next to him. She kicked him in the side, sending waves of agony through him.

"Who was it?" she said.

Victor laughed, tasting blood on his lips. "You don't get it," he said. "They thought...thought you were dead."

"Who?"

"You could have left," he said, gasping from the pain and laughing. "When they find out you are still alive...the will...never...never stop..."

He crawled another step, gasping and coughing.

Kate knelt down, placing the barrel of the gun up to his chin.

"Who was it?" she asked, her voice soft.

Victor gasped for air and leaned forward. "When they...when they find you...tell...tell them...I said..."

Kate pulled the trigger and it ended.

2

The dust cleared and Helen rubbed her eyes, trying to see what happened. She heard yelling and had run to Beck's side as soon as the fight started, making sure he was okay. She heard gunshots, a scuffle and then silence. She didn't know who had come in the car or what had happened.

A second later she did. Her sister walked out of the dust cloud toward her, very much alive. He had a gun in her hand and looked beat up but otherwise okay.

"Kate!" Helen screamed, rushing forward and hugging her sister.

"I'm all right," Kate said, hugging her close. "I'm all right."

"Oh my God, I thought you were dead," Helen said, crying.

"I know," Kate said. "It's okay, I'm here now."

The sound of drones passing overhead interrupted their moment, and Kate held her sister back. "We need to stop those," Kate said.

"We can't," Helen replied, sniffling and rubbing her nose. "The laptop is destroyed. I don't have any other links to their network."

"Then what do we do?"

Helen blew out a shuddering breath. "I don't know."

3

Lyle crawled to his contraption on the roof, leaning against the wall next to his regulator box and finally allowing himself to relax. He had made it, and he'd never been so proud of himself.

He would die knowing he'd done his best.

"Come on Lyle," he muttered. "Stay focused."

The world swam in and out of focus as he fiddled with the regulator. He needed to remove the remote connection and hook up the manual one again, splicing together two wires.

The sound of the approaching planes grew louder. There were sirens in the distance but none of that was any concern. This was the last thing he needed to accomplish. He had hooked the regulator up to high voltage industrial wires, which were around five hundred kilovolts.

If his contraption worked, the EMP released would be massive. If it didn't, the explosion would be even bigger.

He turned, gasping and groaning, and found a position he could watch the approaching drones from. There were several of them, little specks on the horizon getting larger by the second.

It felt peaceful, sitting on the roof and watching it. He heard a bird screech in the distance and felt the wind rustling past his cheeks. The pain was almost entirely gone.

He rested his finger on the switch. If he was about to die, then, at least, he would make it as worthwhile as he could.

4

Kate grabbed the laptop out of her car and handed it to her sister. She knew Lyle had been fiddling with it, and maybe there would be something her sister could do with it.

"Anything you can do?"

"Not really," she said. "We don't have time."

Helen typed furiously, and after a second of loading, an

image popped up on the screen.

"What is that?"

"The live stream," Helen said.

"The what?"

"Six hundred thousand viewers," she read in horror.

"What?"

"Victor wanted to broadcast the attack around the world for everyone to see. There are six hundred thousand people that are about the watch these drones kill several thousand civilians."

"You can't stop it?"

Helen looked at her helplessly. "I'm sorry."

"Damn it," Kate said, leaning heavily against the car. "Damn it all."

She felt like crying. After all of this, she was about to fail in this mission. She had lived her life doing horrible things, and this had been her chance at redemption. At finally doing something good with her life and stopping the people she'd once trusted.

And now she had failed and those people were going to—

"What's that?"

Kate glanced over. "What's what?"

Helen pointed at the screen. "On that roof. It looks like...is that a person?"

Kate looked at the image and saw Lyle, leaning against his contraption on the roof. The drones weren't very far from him, almost right over top of them.

Suddenly, the feed cut out.

"What was that?" Helen asked.

Kate turned and looked back at the building where she had left him. The building the drones were flying over top.

"Uh oh."

She saw the drones falling out of the sky. One smashed into the side of the building, another two went all the way down and hit the ground, exploding into metal and smoke.

The last two smashed into the roof.

A moment passed in silence as the sisters stared in awe.

"What the hell was that?" Helen asked.

Kate turned to face her sister, shocked beyond her wildest dreams.

"Our backup plan."

Epilogue

1

The FBI showed up to the scene in Cottonwood Heights less than an hour after the attack. They flew in by helicopter and came in jeeps, surrounding the area and closing it off for investigation. They found both of the missing Air Force pilots at a local hospital.

Steven Beck was being treated for a gunshot wound to the knee, and Jack was outside, waiting to see if his friend would be okay with a gunshot wound to the shoulder. There was a woman with them named Helen Allison, though they were unable to determine if she was part of the incident or a bystander.

They also found two bodies and a severely wounded man. The man was a known criminal working for an underground mercenary organization known as JanCorp. The two dead men were his associates Victor Cross and Francis Umstead.

In the building where the drones crashed, they found a large amount of blood belonging to their highest priority criminal, Lyle Goldman, but no body. They checked all local hospitals but found no trace of him. They decided with the amount of blood loss he was probably dead.

2

Lyle groaned as he woke up, agony flooding his entire body. Bright light assaulted him from overhead, and he raised his arm to shield his eyes.

"Finally," Kate said, sitting in the chair next to him.

"Finally?" he said. "Is this heaven?"

"Am I in your heaven?"

"If you were, you would be wearing fewer clothes," Lyle

said. Then he paused. "Did I just say that out loud?"

"It's the painkillers," she laughed. "You'll be loopy for a while."

"Where am I?"

"I called in a few favors and got you patched up. Now we're hiding out so you can recover."

"Hiding out?" he asked.

"The FBI is still after you, and you're still a person of interest. There isn't a manhunt anymore. It's died down a little, but it'll be a few weeks before you are off their radar."

"Then things can go back to normal?"

Kate smiled sadly at him.

"No," she said. "Things will never go back to normal. The life you knew is gone. The only thing you can do now is move forward."

Lyle thought about that for a second. "Didn't my plan work?" he asked.

"It did," Kate said. "And you are a hero. But, no one will ever know that except us."

"So I don't get a medal?" he asked, laughing.

She smiled. "No. But how about a consolation prize?"

"Like what?" he asked.

She leaned in and gave him a long and passionate kiss. When she got done he was breathless.

"Yeah," he said. "That works."

"I thought it might."

"What do we do now?" he asked.

"We?"

"You saved me. In some cultures, that makes you responsible for me."

She laughed. "Maybe."

"So, what do we do now?"

"Well," Kate said, leaning back in her chair and smiling. "It just so happens that we've got a new job."

Thank you for reading!

Lincoln Cole

About the Author

Lincoln Cole is a Columbus-based author who enjoys traveling and has visited many different parts of the world, including Australia and Cambodia, but always returns home to his pugamonster puppy, Luther, and family. His love for writing was kindled at an early age through the works of Isaac Asimov and Stephen King and he enjoys telling stories to anyone who will listen.

http://www.LincolnCole.net

CPSIA information can be obtained
at www.ICGtesting.com
Printed in the USA
BVOW03*1847170717
489513BV00001B/1/P